CRUMB AND PUNISHMENT

A KC CRUMB MYSTERY

GEORGIANA DANIELS

Cozy Cove Press

Cover by Dineen Miller

Print ISBN: 978-1-7367250-2-3

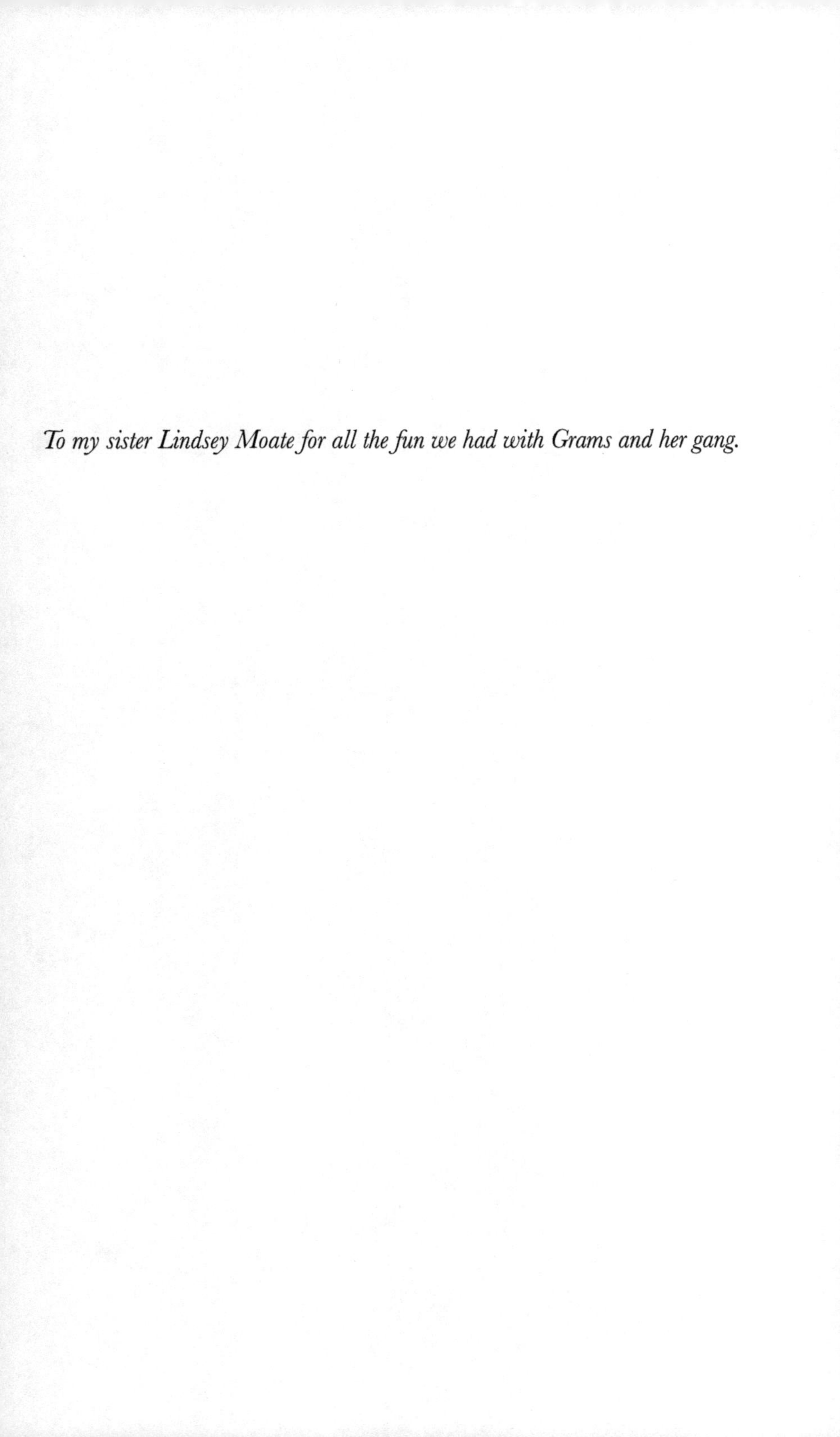

FRIDAY NIGHT BINGO at the Beaver Bluff Senior Center was the last place I expected to be hanging out at this point in my life. It wouldn't have been so bad, except it was the third time this week.

"B-seven, B-seven." Walter, the owner of Yum Yum's Ice Cream Shop, doubled as the caller on bingo nights. Secretly, I think he was looking for love. Unless, there was another reason he snapped his suspenders with glee after my aunt's friend Naomi won the last round.

"Pay attention. You missed one." Aunt Lulu flicked her gray braid over her shoulder. "I can't keep helping you, or I'll lose track of my own numbers."

With four cards, I was having a hard time keeping up. I was not a power player like my aunt and her pals. To be fair, they'd become my friends too. Polly, Naomi, and Verity—along with Aunt Lulu and me—had solved a murder together, and now we were inseparable, even on bingo night when Verity and I were the only ones under sixty.

Quickly, I dotted my card before Walter churned the cage and pulled out the next ball. He waggled his white eyebrows at Naomi before speaking into his head mic. "B-twelve, B-twelve."

Naomi tittered from the other end of the table. If only it were so easy for the rest of us to find love. Both Verity and I were determined not to fall for the next schmuck who came along after the bad relationships we'd both had. She was duped by her would-be groom, and I was replaced by a younger version of myself back in Los Angeles.

But that was the nice thing about being home in Beaver Bluff—I could just be myself, *by* myself, and not feel like I was missing out on the next premier or other big events that required a plus one. Here, bingo night *was* the biggest event, and until I regrouped and got my career back on track, I could relax and enjoy life in the slow lane.

"You missed one." Ruby Maxwell dabbed her dauber on my B-twelve space, which seemed a little presumptuous considering we'd just met this evening. "Honestly, you only have four cards. Keep up."

I tried not to frown. "Thanks for the *advice*."

"It was kindly meant." She seemed unperturbed by my sarcasm. Ruby dabbed three of her six cards when Walter called out N-thirty.

I perused my cards and found one space to mark. "I guess I'm not a bingo whiz like some people."

Ruby primped her silver hair that was twisted in an up-do too fancy for the senior center. "I've been called worse. You'll have to do better than that to get a rise out of me."

Aunt Lulu nudged me from the other side. "Leave her alone and play the game."

"But she dabbed my card," I whispered back. "It was a little rude."

"I dabbed someone's card once, and they ripped my dauber right out of my hand." Verity's stage whisper from two seats over was louder than Walter calling out I-thirty-five.

"You know I can hear you, right?" Ruby stared at all of us. "You might as well just talk about me out loud."

Polly shushed us from the other side of Verity. "I don't want to miss one."

"Oh, good grief." Ruby rolled her eyes.

I studied Ruby from the side. "For what it's worth, I'm sorry for saying something about you dabbing my card. I'm sure you were only trying to help."

"Exactly." The sleeve of the older woman's purple caftan swayed when she shrugged. "That's all I ever do is try to help. Some people misunderstand, but I figure that's their problem."

"B-eight, B-eight," Walter said into his headset, his eyes fixed on Naomi.

Quickly, I dabbed my cards before anyone else could, then spoke to Ruby. "You're right. It is their problem. Maybe everyone should try to give each other the benefit of the doubt." No one knew better than I did about false accusations after I'd been mixed up in the murder of my ex-boyfriend last month.

"That's what I always say." Ruby pointed her dauber at me to punctuate her words. "It's like when I told Melody Thompson about her husband running around on her. You'd think she'd be a little grateful, but *noooo*. She went on and on about staying out of other people's business. And don't you know, that's exactly what I intend to do from now on," she said with a note of pride in her voice that told me she intended no such thing.

"Melody Thompson…her name sounds familiar." I scanned my cards as Walter pulled another number. I was so close to bingo I could taste it, not that winning was all it was cracked up to be. The biggest prize was a coupon to the buffet near the marina down at the cove.

"Melody works at the yarn store, and her soon-to-be-ex-husband owns the sporting goods shop at the town square." Judging by the size of Ruby's eyes when she spoke, she was only too delighted to fill me in on the gritty details. "And that's where I found him with another woman."

I held up my dauber and shook my head. "I don't want to know."

"Apparently, neither did Melody." Ruby guffawed.

I tried to picture Melody from the yarn shop. I'd been there once with Verity so she could pick up a few skeins to knit a baby blanket. Knitting was her biggest hobby after jiu-jitsu. My librarian friend had varied tastes.

"N-thirty, N-thirty." The head mic squealed when Walter called out the number.

"Maybe I don't know her," I said, unable to fill in a square. "I don't get out much since I spend most of my time at Crumb's."

"Isn't that a bakery?" Ruby asked.

"Yeah, my aunt owns it. We have the best croissants in town." My mouth watered, and I could actually feel my waistline expand as I considered the flaky goodness.

"I haven't been there since before my heart surgery. But now that my ticker is back in shape, maybe I'll give it another try."

"You should." I smiled at Ruby, hoping to soften her gruff exterior. "Your first treat is on me."

"G-forty-seven, G-forty-seven."

"Bingo!" Naomi called from the end of the table, raising her arms in victory.

"Again?" Ruby threw down her dauber. "It's rigged. Thanks for nothing, Walter."

A dark look momentarily passed over Walter's face before he angled toward Naomi to verify her win. For her, he was all smiles.

"I'm going to get a coffee before the next round. You want one?" Ruby used her cane to hoist herself off the seat. Her knees cracked in protest.

"I'm good, but thanks." I gathered my cards and squared them against the table.

Aunt Lulu watched Ruby leave. "I'd be careful about saying too much around her."

"Meh, she seems harmless enough." Chatty and completely lacking boundaries, but harmless.

Polly and Verity huddled around Lulu and me while Naomi stayed in her seat, making googly eyes at Walter.

"What's the deal with those two?" I asked the gang. "They weren't like this a few nights ago when we were here."

"You left early, remember? After that, they started talking, and the next day Naomi spent an hour at the ice cream shop." Verity's eyes took on a dreamy quality. "I think it's love."

I jostled her shoulder to shake her out of her reverie. "We don't believe in that lovey-dovey stuff. Remember?"

"You're right. It's all a crock." Disappointment laced Verity's voice.

"Would you two knock it off?" Polly glanced between the two of us. "Just because you met a few screwballs doesn't mean every nut in the barn is bad."

Aunt Lulu tilted her head. "I'm not sure how many metaphors Polly just mixed there, but she has a point. When the time is right, it'll happen for both of you."

I tamped down the urge to argue, mostly because I wanted to believe they were right, even if I never saw evidence of real love anywhere around me. Except for maybe my parents, who loved each other enough to stay married for five thousand years, but *only* had enough love for each other and none to share with me. That was probably why they'd left me with my aunt so many years ago.

I cleared the melancholy from my head before I spoke. "Maybe I need a cup of coffee after all. Once we're done here, I still have some work to do at home."

Aunt Lulu beamed with pride as she spoke to the gang. "She already made my website all snazzy, and now she's working on my grand reopening." Her eyes slivered playfully. "Not that I really think I need one since we never actually closed."

"You don't have to have closed. Businesses do them all the time after they update themselves and rebrand. It'll be fun." I nudged her with my elbow. "When everyone sees your grand reopening, they'll all want one. It'll be a nice way for me to get a little consulting business going and help others with their promotions."

After losing my job as a social media manager for a large shoe company in LA, I'd taken on rebranding my aunt's business, Crumb's Bakery. While it was small potatoes compared to what I'd done in the past, the job was satisfying in a way nothing else had been, probably because I was working for someone I loved.

I stood and pushed in my chair. "If I find a few clients, maybe I'll stay in Beaver Bluff a little longer."

Polly clasped her hands, eyes wide. "I know someone who might need you. She was just saying the other day how she needs some marketing help with her animal rescue. I'll tell Trudi to stop by."

"Thank you. I'd love to help our little furry friends find homes." My heart turned soft as I thought of my dog, Pooh Bear, who still needed a walk tonight before I started working on projects. "Anyone else want coffee?"

Angry voices sounded from the refreshment area in the hall. I hurried to check it out. Several people hovered close, coffee cups in hand, watching.

"I can't go anywhere without running into you." A woman with curly brown hair and wild eyes loomed over Ruby, who leaned on the snack table to support herself. Like me, she seemed a little young to be at the senior center, but there was only so much one could do on a Friday night in Beaver Bluff.

"I was here first, so I suggest you quit following me." Ruby shook her cane at the lady.

"No one is following you. I came here for bingo, just like everyone else." Rage seeped off the woman in waves. "But no, you just have to be a busybody all over the place."

"How dare you!" Ruby responded with equal venom.

"Gran, maybe we should leave." A dark-haired man about my age attempted to clasp Ruby's shoulders to guide her away, but she shook him off.

"I'm staying put." Ruby wagged her cane at the other woman again.

The lady smacked the cane, and it clattered to the floor. Then she turned and stormed out the door of the senior center, leaving behind a wake of disbelief.

"Well, I never," Ruby said with disgust. She angrily brushed the front of her caftan.

Ruby's grandson bent over and retrieved the cane. "Are you sure you don't want to go home?" He lowered his voice. "It's almost time for your meds."

She grabbed her cane and planted it on the floor. "It's just as well. I think Walter rigged this ridiculous game. Imagine the same person winning all night just because she's making eyes at him."

Anger flared inside me. How dare Ruby speak about Naomi that way! Naomi, who never hurt anyone or cheated on anything a day in her life. Maybe the gang was right about staying away from Ruby. Too bad I'd already invited her to Crumb's.

Ruby lifted her chin, then hobbled toward the door. The young man spoke in a placating tone as he guided her out the entrance. Everyone in the hall looked at each other, then quietly resumed their own conversations.

"What was all that about?" Polly smoothed her pageboy haircut as she watched the door swing shut.

Verity gathered us close, her green eyes wide. "That was Ella from the bistro. She seemed pretty upset with Ruby."

"The bistro at the town square?" Naomi joined our group. "I heard they're closing shop."

Polly snapped her fingers. "Drat, just when I found a pasta I like. Seems like they just opened a few months ago. It's a shame Ella couldn't make it work."

"You haven't heard?" Aunt Lulu frowned. "I thought everyone in town knew."

"Knew what?" All of a sudden, I felt like an outsider again.

Aunt Lulu leaned into the huddle. "There were issues with the health department. I'm no stranger to inspections—they can be brutal—but something just doesn't seem right about how it all went down. From everything I heard, Ella ran a tight ship."

"The health department came in for a reason." Verity glanced around to ensure no one else was listening. "There was an incident of food poisoning."

"What?" Polly broke all pretense of secrecy. "That can't be right. Ella's place is the best in town."

Verity motioned for her to come back into the tight circle. "I don't know whether or not it's true, but I do know that it was you-know-who who got the ball rolling to shut her down."

"Who?" I asked.

Verity spoke in a somber tone. "Ruby Maxwell."

Chapter Two

THERE'S a reason people in food photography don't use actual food, and it probably has something to do with eating the props.

Aunt Lulu fisted her hands on her hips as she gazed up at me. "That was your third raspberry cream puff."

"Fourth, but who's counting?" Polly licked her finger to turn the page of the magazine she perused nearby.

The thin afternoon crowd at Crumb's spread out over the cozy bakery, and upbeat pop tunes played softly in the background. This was my favorite time of day—the quiet after the rush when the smell of freshly baked goods still lingered in the air. The sounds and smells of my childhood were oddly comforting in this transitional season of my life.

I repositioned myself on top of the chair, precariously balanced over a table near the window. The lighting was good, but the cream puffs lacked the perfection needed to get a quality shot. Maybe if I took one more out of the pile…

"You said you wanted to take pictures, but instead, you're eating the whole batch." The dismay in Lulu's voice kept me from snatching the extra puff.

"It's not like you were going to put these back in the case." I leaned over and adjusted the props next to the puffs, ignoring snickering patrons at the adjacent table. "Besides, I'm just trying to get the best pictures possible to put on your social channels."

"What's all that social mumbo jumbo supposed to do?" Naomi, with her puffy white hair, peered up at me quizzically.

I snapped a few shots before responding. "By taking great pictures and posting them with strategic hashtags, we'll gain more traction and thus, more excitement for the grand reopening." I adjusted the puffs one more time, then hunched over the camera again to get another photo.

"That reminds me," Polly said as she turned another page. "I gave your phone number to my friend. She sounded interested in getting your help to ramp up all her…whatever it is you do."

Carefully, I angled the camera and took another picture. "Trudi texted me this morning. She's going to meet me here, at some point." Poor lady definitely needed help. She only had the same two or three people liking her posts.

Naomi held up her hand. "That reminds me, the theater group needs a little help, too. One of the gals told me last night they have a production coming up and need some marketing help."

I could only hope they weren't paying me in free tickets. Even though I had a decent savings account, I needed to start earning money again at some point.

"Looks like you're living dangerously." The sonorous voice nearly toppled me. Officer Antonio Hamson stood next to Lulu. He wore a plain polo shirt that stretched across his muscular chest and had his sunglasses tucked into the V of his collar.

"Officer"—I refused to say his last name, lest I screw it up and call him Handsome instead of Hamson—"haven't seen you around much."

Hamson had the decency to look sheepish. After the gang and I had solved the last mystery, Hamson had only stopped by the bakery a handful of times, at least while I was working. Whatever tiny flicker of hope I'd had that the officer and I could be anything more than casual acquaintances had been snuffed out. What hadn't been snuffed out, unfortunately, was the way my pulse skittered at the sight of his classically dark features, broad shoulders, and eyes like twin pools of hot fudge.

I steadied myself on the table and climbed off the chair, trying not to show how flustered I was at Hamson's sudden appearance.

"Yeah, where ya been?" Polly set down her magazine, then motioned to me. "Did little missy here do something to chase you off?"

"Polly!" Lulu, Naomi, and I chastised her at the same time.

"What'd I say?" Her gaze bounced between us.

Hamson appeared unflustered. "It's been busy down at the station. I've been working a lot of night shifts, too."

"But a man still has to eat," Naomi said sweetly. "Don't tell us you found another place."

"He did. I saw him at the bistro." Polly narrowed her eyes at him.

"You know, Polly, that means you were eating there too." Lulu pulled a shaker out of her apron pocket and added sprinkles to the puffs, giving them a nice pop of color. "Let's not give Antonio a hard time now, okay? I'm sure he has his reasons for taking his business elsewhere." She winked at him, eliciting one in return.

"You ladies know I love Crumb's. I just felt bad that the bistro is closing up, so I've had a few meals there." He offered a good-natured shrug. It was nice to see his softer, non-police-y side for once.

"We were talking about that last night at bingo." Naomi scooted her chair closer to Hamson, then spoke in a conspiratorial tone. "We all saw a fight between the bistro owner and another lady."

Hamson turned to me and cocked a grin. "Playing bingo at the senior center now, KC?"

Heat crept into my cheeks. It was beyond me why it mattered

what the officer thought about my social life—or lack of one, more specifically. I was my own woman. So what if I enjoyed a rousing game of bingo every now and then? I matched his grin. "It's a perfectly good way to spend a Friday evening."

"I'm sure it is. So, tell me about this brawl." Already he was slipping back into cop mode.

"It wasn't a brawl, per se, just two ladies arguing." I fiddled with the cream puff display to hide the nerves that jittered every time I interacted with the police. Or maybe it was this one officer in particular. I dropped the puff and headed toward the counter where Krystal, the part-time employee I'd once thought could be a murderer, was helping another customer. "How about a bagel?"

"Sounds good." Hamson followed me, then waited until Krystal and the other customer were out of earshot before speaking again. "Who was Ella arguing with?"

"Oh, you're on a first-name basis with her."

His eyebrow peaked. "It's Beaver Bluff. Everyone is on a first-name basis."

"Anyway, Ella had it out with Ruby somebody-or-other, a lady I met last night." I donned a pair of gloves and reached for a garlic bagel inside the case.

Hamson motioned to the scant choices left. "Just a plain one today."

"Plain? That's a first. Seeing someone special later?" I bit my tongue, irritated with myself for making it sound like I cared, which I most definitely did not.

His mouth quirked. "Define special."

"Never mind. I was just teasing." Not flirting—two totally different things. I slipped the bagel inside a paper sleeve and handed it over the counter. "This one is on the house. Maybe you'll start coming back again. I know the gang misses you."

"*Just* the gang?" Hamson pulled a few bills out of his wallet and stuffed them into the tip jar. He refused to meet my eye. Something was up, but I didn't want to ask.

"You know the ladies here—creatures of habit. They enjoy talking to the regulars." I laughed it off to sound casual. "Cream cheese?"

"Please."

I grabbed a packet from the cooler and handed it over. "Thanks for stopping by. Come again." I walked around the counter into the dining area.

Hamson quickstepped beside me. "Wait, you haven't finished telling me about last night."

Frankly, I didn't think it was all that interesting. I shrugged. "Apparently, that Ruby lady accused the bistro owner—"

"Ella."

"Yeah, Ella." I paused and considered her. She'd appeared to be a little younger than me and kind of adorable—when she wasn't yelling at Ruby. Was it possible Hamson had a thing for her, and that's why he kept quizzing me? I shook off the thought. It was none of my business, and I didn't care. Much.

"Go on…"

I studied Hamson, noting the concern in his eyes. "Ruby accused Ella of following her. The gang seems to think that Ruby has something to do with the bistro closing down."

Hamson grumbled under his breath.

"You seem awfully interested in what happened." I searched his face for telltale signs of…I wasn't sure what. "Why do you care what happened at the senior center?"

"As an officer, it's important that I stay on top of everything that goes on."

"Okay, Barney."

Hamson grimaced. "As in Fife?"

"If the badge fits." I snickered. Bright yellow fabric caught my attention outside the window. A caftan, which could only mean one thing. "Speak of the devil—here comes Ruby now."

Hamson turned his gaze to the window. "That's Ruby?"

I nodded. If only I could retract my invitation. The last thing I wanted was to give the grouch a free croissant. For all I knew, she could try to turn Crumb's in to the health department for a violation like she did with the bistro or start rumors that affected the business.

Hamson pulled his sunglasses off the collar of his shirt and slid them over his eyes. "That's my cue to leave." He looked toward the gang and toasted them with his bagel. "Ladies."

"Don't be a stranger," Polly called after him as he breezed out the door. She shot a look at Ruby, who had yet to enter the bakery, then turned to me. "I'm leaving too."

"Me, three." Naomi rose from her seat and followed Polly toward the door. They awkwardly exchanged harrumphs with Ruby as she used her cane to bully past them to get inside.

Ruby sure knew how to clear a room.

I pasted on my most gracious smile as she and her grandson approached the counter. "It's great to see you again." I nearly choked on the lie. Ever since getting to know Verity and her penchant for telling the truth in all circumstances, it was getting harder for me to even offer phony pleasantries.

Ruby hiked her thumb over her shoulder. "What's with the mass exodus?" Then she snickered. "That doesn't bode well for your pastries if you know what I mean." She glanced around the half-empty room. "Am I right?"

Thankfully, a phone trilled inside her purse, which was carried by the young man instead of Ruby. He pulled it out and looked at the faceplate. "You'll need to take this. It's Benson."

She grabbed the phone and stepped away from the counter, but close enough for me to hear her brusque side of the conversation. I felt a little bad for her grandson, who seemed like a nice enough guy.

"Sorry about that." He cringed. "I mean about what she said. I'm sure your pastries are great." Embarrassment swept over his handsome face as he set her giant handbag on the counter. "Gran sometimes says things she shouldn't."

"It's fine." Another lie. Verity would be so disappointed.

He glanced at his grandmother, who droned on. "I hope I didn't forget to write an appointment in her book."

"It looks like you do a lot for her. I'm sure she appreciates it." I switched subjects before I could stretch the truth any further. "What can I get for you today? It's on the house."

Lulu grimaced across the room.

Before the guy could answer, Ruby piped in. "I want to try one of those scones." She pointed to the raspberry ones in the case. "I wasn't talking to you, Benson." She barked into her phone. "If that's the case, I think my money would do better elsewhere. Clearly, they don't need it."

The young man cringed again. He drew a breath and perused the case. "Maybe just a coffee for me, thanks."

"Coming right up." I filled a to-go cup with coffee, then bagged the scone while Ruby stepped to the side and droned on about some financial issue. I handed the goods over.

Ruby's grandson leaned against the counter and took a sip. "Great coffee. It hits the spot."

"It's a special roast." I inhaled the rich scent and watched the guy watch Ruby. "It's nice that you get to spend a lot of time with your grandmother. By the way, I'm KC."

"David." He took another drink. "Nice to meet you. I saw you at bingo."

"I'd have done better to stay home. I can't get a bingo to save my life."

"I hear you. There's not much else to do in town, though." He offered a slim smile before glancing over his shoulder at Ruby.

"All I'm saying is, I don't want to play games with it." She rolled her eyes as though it was, in fact, a game to her—whatever *it* was.

"You're right. If there was anything else to do besides bingo, I'd be doing it." I wiped down the counter.

David grinned. "You're telling me. It's okay, though. For me, it's important to spend time with Gran while I still have her." He leaned closer and spoke just above a whisper. "Besides, she isn't always so…*gruff.*"

Just then, Ruby disconnected and groaned before tossing the phone into her purse. Then she picked up the scone, slid it out of the bag, and took a bite. "Hmm, it's okay, I guess," she said, crumbs dotting her mouth. "But probably not worth bragging about."

Chapter Three

THE FACT that flour dotted Aunt Lulu's nose did not detract from her serious tone. "For the last time, I don't think we need to do all these extra things you're talking about."

"Let me just make a mockup, a sample to show you what the catering menu would look like. It'll be good with the grand reopening." I held up a little drawing I'd sketched a few minutes earlier after my official shift at the front counter was over. "Everyone should get a chance to experience Crumb's, and it would give you an opportunity to expand—"

"I don't want to ex—"

"We could even get into merchandise. It would be like a Crumb's empire." Excitement lit inside me just thinking of digging my hands into a project this size, the way I had back in LA when our company would launch a new line.

"I don't want to build an empire." A trench formed between Lulu's gray eyebrows, and her lips clamped.

"Maybe a small chain?"

"I don't want to be a chain. I'm happy with the way things are. Let's just stick to a small reopening." Lulu's voice softened as she patted my shoulder. "Look, I know you're getting a little restless, but expanding the business to epic proportions is not the answer."

"Fine," I groaned. "But I think you're missing a lot of opportunities."

"I like Crumb's the way it is." She flicked her hands at me. "Now shoo. Krystal and I are going to close the kitchen down so we can head to the town square."

I tucked the drawing into my handbag, did an about-face, and went back out onto the floor. Verity waved at me through the window, where she stood outside with Pooh Bear. The sight of my trusty canine sent a wave of gratitude through me. Though I'd never considered owning a pet before, Verity had made a smart move by pairing me up with the giant German shepherd after my rental had been broken into. Now, I couldn't imagine life without him—never mind that he used my hundred-dollar slippers as a chew toy.

I went outside and crouched next to him, earning myself a furry nuzzle. "How is my little love bug, Pooh Bear?"

"Are you ready? I want to scope out some of the booths before they close." Verity handed me the leash.

The briny scent of the ocean blew in from the bluff across the street, and heavy clouds loomed overhead. A slight chill in the air reminded me that fall was here. We set off toward the town square, Pooh Bear muscling his way down the sidewalk. For a moment, I wished I'd worn sneakers rather than kitten heels, considering my dog kept a much faster pace than me.

"Are you looking for something in particular?" I slid on my sunglasses as we rounded the corner and headed for the heart of Beaver Bluff.

Today was the last day of the craft fair, and there were at least fifty tents filled with paintings, jewelry, woodwork, and custom hats and t-shirts. Of course, there was also a row of food—flavored popcorn, gyros, a taco truck, and fried donuts—but I had my sight set on Yum Yum's. Ice cream was a hard habit to break.

"There's a vendor who specializes in Bigfoot paraphernalia,

and I want to see if they have any new merchandise." The breeze ruffled Verity's red hair. "But we can definitely get ice cream first. Hey, there's Officer Hamson." She pointed indiscreetly.

I pulled her arm down before she attracted his attention. Hamson strolled out the front door of the bistro with Officer Leon, his female partner whose eyelashes I was not coveting… much. "Looks like he's got her hooked on the Bistro at the Bluffs food, too."

Verity gave me the side-eye. "And what's wrong with that, exactly?"

"Nothing," I said too quickly. "He can eat anywhere he wants. What's it to me?"

She snorted. "Jealous?"

"Absolutely not. I'm sure Ella has fantastic…" I waved my hand around. "Whatever it is, she serves. Never mind the allegations of food poisoning." We stopped in front of the ice cream shop, and I handed over Pooh Bear's leash. "You two wait here, and I'll grab our ice creams. You want the usual?"

"That'd be great."

Pooh Bear gazed up at me with his sappy brown eyes and grunted. I pawed through my purse for a doggie treat, which he promptly snatched. I patted his head. "Be right back." Inside, soft music played to an audience of none—I wasn't even sure the owner was in. "Walter, are you here?"

Walter ambled out of the back room. "Well, if it isn't KC, one of my favorite people in all of Beaver Bluff."

"I bet you say that to all the ladies." I tittered as I approached the counter.

He snapped his red suspenders. "Only the sweetest of the sweet."

"I know a certain lady who would love to hear that, herself." I waggled my eyebrows and thought of Naomi, who seemed head over heels for this gentleman.

"Really?" Walter leaned back, genuine surprise lighting his face. "And who might that be?"

"Oh, I think you know." I tapped the counter to punctuate each word. "Maybe the next time you see her, you could suggest a little night out on the town next weekend."

He rubbed the white whiskers on his chin. "I don't know about that."

"Why not?"

A serious look camped in his eyes. "Well, you know I'm the bingo caller down at the senior center. I'm not sure I could neglect my responsibilities. The good folks of Beaver Bluff are counting on me every weekend."

"Indeed, they are." I decided not to push too hard. Instead, I perused the ice cream selection.

"What'll you have today? The usual?" Walter reached for a pair of plastic gloves.

It was a little disappointing that I even *had* a usual, considering I hadn't eaten ice cream the entire decade before returning home. Since I'd come back, there was more than one spot in town— excluding Ella's bistro—that knew my order by heart. I smiled. "The usual would be fine, for Verity and me both."

Walter set to work on our order. "What are the two of you up to on this fine afternoon?"

"We're heading across the street to check out some vendors. I'll probably do a little more work later tonight."

"What kind of work might that be?" Walter plopped a scoop onto a waffle cone.

"I'm helping my aunt with her grand reopening and maybe a little social media work for some others." I glanced around his shop, my head filling with ideas. "Maybe I could even come up with something for you."

He nodded thoughtfully. "Let me think on that. In the meantime, I'll bet Ella next door at the bistro could use some help in that department."

For some reason, her name was like nails on a chalkboard to me. I cringed. "From what I hear, it's too late to save her restaurant."

"That it is, that it is. But," Walter said, a spark in his voice. "I hear she's starting something else under a new name. Maybe you could give her a hand. She's a right, nice lady."

I worked hard not to roll my eyes. What kind of voodoo had Ella used to charm everyone? Quickly, I smiled to cover my uncharitable thoughts. "I'll keep that in mind."

We continued to chat as I watched Pooh Bear dominate the sidewalk. His solid build and the alertness of his ears made people wary, but Verity seemed to have a good handle on him for the moment. Then I paid for the ice cream.

Walter handed me a few napkins and grinned. "I expect to see you again soon. If it wasn't for you, I might not be in the black this month."

"Now that tourist season is over, I think we're all slowing down." I took the first nibble of the creamy goodness.

"Could definitely do with a little more business. You know how that goes."

"Amen to that. Anyhoo, remember what I said. I can help you during the slow season, and I'll give you the family discount." I toasted him with my cone.

A dark look crossed his face as his eyes traveled past me. He grumbled under his breath, and the only word I could make out was "wretched," which was practically a swear word for Walter.

I turned around and immediately understood. Ruby stood outside the shop, this time sporting a floral caftan that billowed in the breeze. She leaned over slightly, her hand poised above Pooh Bear's head. I cringed, knowing what was coming but not daring to look away.

He barked.

Ruby jumped.

"Naughty, Pooh Bear." Verity's firm voice carried through the window.

Ruby's face purpled. She flung open the door and hobbled inside, her cane bumping along quickly. "Well, I never." Disgust laced her words. "Honestly, if people can't control their mangy pets, they should keep them at home."

I was too startled to claim Pooh Bear.

"You here for a little afternoon treat, Ruby?" The levity in my tone deserved an award.

She noticed me for the first time since walking in, and her mood lightened, if only a little. "Indeed. I thought it would hit the spot. My stomach's been a little upset ever since I had that scone at your place last week."

My fists clenched.

Walter started to mumble again, so I tried to drown him out. "Walter just loves when people stop in for ice cream." Or at least he should since he apparently needed the business. I glanced out the window for David, who seemed to go every-where with Ruby. Instead, I just saw Pooh Bear sitting calmly on his haunches, watching people go by. "So, Ruby…where's your grandson?"

She waved dismissively. "He's somewhere out there. He'll be in soon, I guess." She grimaced, then glanced around. "I'm supposed to meet someone here. Looks like they're late, as usual."

Walter grumbled a not-nice word that I attempted to cover with a cough. "That sounds great. Well…see you around." I hustled out the door and handed Verity her cone before it dripped on me. "Let's get out of here."

"Can I finish my cone first?" She scooted over and made room on the bench. Pooh Bear inched over with her.

"Sure. I just don't want another run-in with you-know-who."

"No, who?" Verity's eyes widened.

I jerked my head toward the shop. "Ruby. She's totally in a mood today."

"That's every day."

"You're not wrong." I licked my mint chocolate chip before it dripped onto my fingers. "The weird thing is, Walter seems to have a problem with her, too."

Verity laughed sardonically. "You know it's bad if the ice

cream man doesn't like you. Pooh Bear wasn't too crazy about her, either." He woofed in agreement, startling a jogger in the road.

Instead of worrying about running into Ruby again, I eased back on the bench and listened to the music coming from a stage in the middle of the square. A local band crooned about lost love and lost wages, with a surprisingly upbeat melody considering the subject matter. Several people hovered near the band, and others milled between the tents and under the trees, whose leaves had started to change. I relaxed a fraction, thankful for the peaceful day.

"This is the life, isn't it?" Verity finished up her cone. "I mean, I know you're missing the big city, but Los Angeles can't compare to—"

A gunshot rang out.

I stood. Pooh Bear barked. The crowd screamed and scattered.

"Help! Someone, anyone!" A voice cried from behind the taco truck. "My husband accidentally shot himself!"

Pooh Bear bolted toward the action.

I hustled after him, trying to grab the leash, but each time I came close, he went faster. "Pooh Bear, come back!" My ankles wobbled as I ran in heels. Verity's footsteps sounded behind me.

The crowd that had just dispersed slowly came back together. Pooh Bear aimed right at them. When he reached the periphery, he barked again. People jumped back, and some yelled obscenities. Finally, I grabbed his leash and shushed him, even as others crowded in behind me. Some bystanders had their cell phones out to video the scene.

"What happened?" Verity pushed her way through the throng of onlookers.

I peered between the sea of legs and spotted a man rolling on the ground, writhing in pain. He cried out, even as his frantic wife crouched at his side, offering comfort.

Verity whipped her phone out of her back pocket. "I'm calling nine-one-one. We'll get an ambulance here."

Just then, Hamson and Officer Leon pushed through the crowd. "Police, coming through," he said, making his way to the action. "What happened?"

"My husband was showing off his gun, and pow!" The wife threw her arms out for emphasis. "I told him that would happen. He doesn't even know how to use the thing." Her arms waved frantically. "I think he shot his toe off!"

Judging by the blood pooling at his feet, it was highly possible.

"Oww. I think I'm dying." The man rolled in time with his words.

"Don't panic. Help is on the way." Hamson knelt next to him for a closer look. "How did this happen?"

"I told him to make sure the thing wasn't loaded before we came today, but he just had to show off his antique gun." The wife's concern was laced with chastisement.

The man running the antiques booth adjacent to the victim simply shrugged.

Officer Leon spoke to the crowd. "Okay, everyone. Time to move on. The show is over."

Slowly, the crowd began to disperse, but a few of the more brazen folks continued to video the episode.

Just then, Walter came up behind me, sweat beading at his hairline. He was out of breath when he spoke. "What on earth happened here? Is that Charlie?"

The wife glanced up. "He accidentally shot himself."

Walter wiped his brow and ambled toward Charlie. "We need to get him some help."

Apparently, Hamson didn't count.

Sirens sounded in the distance. Officer Leon cut Walter off before he could reach the injured man. "Everyone back away. We'll handle this from here. Go on, now." She flicked her hands at us. "That includes you, KC."

Pooh Bear barked at her. Officer Leon met his glare, causing my dog to whimper. I tugged his leash. "Let's go."

"I'll give you a call tonight," Walter said to Charlie. Then he turned to us as he continued to pant. "That gave me quite a scare."

Verity came alongside him. "Are you okay? We'll walk you back to the shop." She looped her arm through his and led him slowly across the road. Pooh Bear and I followed while I finished the last of my cone. Despite the tragedy, there was no use in letting good ice cream go to waste.

Once we reached Yum Yum's, Walter pulled his arm back and tipped an imaginary hat. "Thank you, lovely ladies."

"Let us at least get you inside." I wrapped Pooh Bear's leash around the base of the bench, then I opened the door.

The shop was eerily still. I stepped aside to let Walter pass, but he stopped. Gasped. Clutched his chest.

I followed his gaze, suddenly remembering there had been someone else inside the shop. It took mere moments to process what I saw. Shock and horror ricocheted inside my chest. A scream tore from my throat.

Ruby lay face-down on the table with a rope cinched tightly around her neck.

Chapter Four

"RUBY!" I ran to her side, my heart catching in my throat.

"Wait! Don't touch her." Verity grabbed my arm just before I reached the older woman. "You might contaminate the scene."

"But she might still be alive." Gently, I tugged free from my friend, then I felt the part of Ruby's neck not covered by the rope.

Walter crept closer. "Well?"

I glanced up and shook my head. "Nothing." My hand trembled as I pulled away. The sight of Ruby's face—discolored by both lack of oxygen and hot fudge—unsettled me. What were the odds of me finding two dead bodies? My stomach roiled as I considered the violence done to Ruby.

"We need to back up." Verity stretched out her arms and herded us away from the body. "Walter, I think you should lock the door before anyone else comes in." I motioned to the kids heading towards the shop, who appeared undeterred by Pooh Bear. Walter made his way to the door, turned the lock, and then flipped the sign from open to closed. The collective groan of the kids was audible through the glass.

"Maybe we should *all* wait outside." Verity rubbed her arms. "And someone should call the police."

"Wait." I held up my hand to stop her. "Let's at least take a closer look before the cops get here."

"Why?" Walter's voice quivered.

I scanned the area and took a few steps back towards the body, trying to gather my wits. "I'm just thinking about what happened last time. The cops basically did nothing to solve the murder. The whole thing was left up to us." I motioned between Verity and myself. "All I'm saying is, it might be a good idea to observe a few details before they show up."

"Think for a second." Panic camped in Walter's eyes. "It doesn't look right, us being in here with a dead body."

"KC, I get what you're saying, but I agree with Walter." Verity backed away while simultaneously reaching into her pocket for her cell. "I'm calling the police."

"Fine." Quickly, I zeroed in on Ruby and her surroundings. There had to be clues here, even if they weren't immediately visible to the naked eye. I resisted the urge to pull out my phone and take a picture but instead attempted to catalog the scene in my brain. Everything in the shop was normal—music playing over the speakers, cash register unopened, chairs pushed neatly under the tables. All of it was just as we'd left it, aside from Ruby.

Her body slumped over the table, her face mashed in her tipped-over ice cream, her dead stare aimed at us. Though a thin blue rope dangled loosely from her neck, it had presumably been tight enough at some point to strangle her. A Louis Vuitton handbag sat next to her sandaled feet and appeared undisturbed. Just as I started to scan the area next to Ruby's handbag, Verity yanked my arm and dragged me away. If I didn't comply, she'd break out her jiu-jitsu moves.

Verity rushed Walter and me out the door, which he locked as quickly as he could with shaky hands. Stragglers on the sidewalk seemed none the wiser about the disturbing scene inside. As long as no one peered through the window, we could avoid a crowd collecting around the ice cream shop the same way it had around the nitwit who'd shot his foot.

"Look, there's Officer Hamson now." Verity frantically waved her arms, attracting the attention I'd just been hoping to avert. "Help, over here!"

Hamson and Officer Leon sauntered across the road, unflustered by Verity's demeanor. Officer Leon spoke first, her voice gentle and calm. "Is everything okay?"

I shushed Verity before she could say anything, then motioned to the shop. "Let's step inside. Walter, will you please unlock the door?" I flashed a false smile at the people hovering on the sidewalk between us and the bistro next door.

Verity smoothed the front of her flannel shirt and spoke with a decidedly unnatural voice. "Yes, let's go inside where we can get out of the...*outdoors*."

Walter's hand was still shaky, and it took two tries before he finally inserted the key into the lock. Hamson peeled off his sunglasses and gave me a questioning look that made my breath hitch. I answered him with a slight shake of my head.

Officer Leon followed Walter inside, then Verity. Hamson's hand grazed the small of my back as he allowed me to step in front of him. As soon as the five of us were behind the closed door, I twisted the lock. A woman outside cupped her hands against the glass to peer at us. Pooh Bear barked, sending the woman away.

"What on earth happened here?" The shock on Officer Leon's face matched what I felt inside.

Seeing the body all over again shook me to the core. Still, I stepped closer and glanced between the officers and Ruby. "After the gunshot incident across the street, we came back and found her."

Hamson's eyes narrowed. "I assume she wasn't like this when you left."

"Of course not—" I stopped just short of calling him Sherlock. I didn't want to be on the wrong side of the investigation like last time.

"KC's right. This is exactly how we found her when we came back." Verity glanced between the officers. "It was just the three of us, and when we walked in, KC screamed."

"That's not important to the story," I said, cutting her off.

"I'm calling this in." Hamson stepped away from me and spoke into the radio clipped to his shoulder while Officer Leon herded us toward the front of the shop.

"I'm going to need you all to stand back until we figure out where we can take your statements." She motioned to the large windows. "Can you close the blinds? The last thing we need is people shooting video before I can clear the scene."

"Good idea." Walter ambled to the window and shooed away more people who had gathered. He rolled down the flimsy shades, then practically collapsed at the nearest table.

"Are you all right?" I hurried to his side. "Can I get you some water?"

"I'll be fine." The sheen on his forehead said otherwise.

Hamson pinched the bridge of his nose and exhaled. "The crime techs are on their way."

"I hope they're more competent than last time." The words were out before I could censor myself. I sat next to Walter and hoped the officers hadn't heard.

Officer Leon nailed me with an inquisitive gaze. "That's right. You were there for the last suspicious death, too."

A sick feeling pummeled my stomach, but I crossed my legs and twirled my foot in an effort to look relaxed. "Apparently, I have a knack for being in the wrong place at the wrong time." I glanced at everyone in the room and offered a thin chuckle. "Am I right, or am I right?"

No one laughed.

Officer Leon's right eyebrow quirked. "As soon as we secure the scene, I'll interview you first."

BEING INTERVIEWED first wasn't all it was cracked up to be. Being interviewed inside the Bistro at the Bluffs was even worse than that. Ella had ever so graciously offered the use of her stockroom-cum-office to Hamson, and he seemed eager to take her up on it. It was, however, better than retelling the story with an audience on the sidewalk.

The desk fan inside the windowless room hummed, occasionally sending spicy notes of aftershave in my direction. I eyed the back door to the right of the desk, wondering if I could make a break for it into the alley rather than having to endure questioning from Hamson. His silence made me nervous.

I picked up a pen and twirled it through my fingers like a baton. "I thought Officer Leon would be doing the interviews."

Hamson glanced up from the notepad in his hand and met me with a cool gaze. "She's working the scene until the state police get here if that's all right with you."

"What's that supposed to mean?" I stopped twirling.

His dark eyes connected with mine. "You can leave the detecting to us this time."

I dropped the pen and met his stare. "I'd feel a lot more comfortable with that if you'd done a good job the *last* time."

Hamson flinched.

"Oh, I get it." I picked up the pen and pointed it at him. "You're upset that I'm the one who solved the murder. That's why you've been standoffish this last month. I stole your thunder."

"That's not it at all—"

"Ah-ha! So, you admit you've been standoffish."

"I admit nothing."

"Look, just because I figured out who the killer was last time doesn't mean you're not somewhat good at your job, and it doesn't mean we can't be friends." *Or more.* I mentally kicked myself for thinking it. "It just means I had a vested interest and a few tricks up my sleeve."

He scoffed and muttered under his breath.

"Whatever you have to say, you can say out loud."

Hamson leaned in so close I could feel his breath when he spoke, momentarily breaking his cop-like disposition. "I said, I'm not having this conversation."

I started twirling the pen again. "Looks like you just did."

The whir of the fan did nothing to drown out his frustrated breaths. At least I now understood why he hadn't been coming around, and I could stop taking it personally. Unless he really did have a thing for the bistro lady, and that was—

Stop it! Thinking about Hamson this way was ridiculous. Considering my track record with men, I was better off alone. Besides, I had my sweet little Pooh Bear to keep me company, and he was more reliable than any man I'd ever known.

Hamson raked his hand through his thick black hair before speaking again. "Take me through it once more. You, Verity, and Walter ran across the street when you heard the gunshot, then...."

"Not exactly." I pictured the scene from the beginning. "Verity and I were already outside, then we ran across the street, following Pooh Bear after the gun went off."

I glanced around the sparsely decorated office. "We were all across the street until you and Officer Leon started clearing the scene. Then we all came back and went inside Yum Yum's. And there was Ruby, dead."

Hamson scrutinized me. "You knew the victim?"

"Uh...not really." Suddenly, I didn't like the way he was looking at me, all suspicious-like. "You knew her too, I thought. She's the same lady I was telling you about at Crumb's the other day, and you left when she walked in."

He slapped his notepad down on the desk. "That's why she seemed familiar."

"You didn't realize that?" I snorted. "You're going to have to up your game."

Hamson scowled, and darn it all, if he wasn't still good-looking...in a platonic sort of way. He cleared his throat. "Did you notice anything else when you got back to the ice cream shop?"

"Everything looked just like it had when we left." I mentally took myself back to the scene and the sudden shock that came over me when we came inside. "Except for Ruby. I noticed that she was strangled with a blue rope and her handbag was still there." I snapped my finger, accidentally flicking the pen and hitting Hamson's chest. "Sorry, I just realized that it means it wasn't a random robbery."

"I told you already you need to leave the investigating to us. Trust me, once the state police get here, they'll slap the cuffs on you if you obstruct the process."

"Obstruct? Who, me?"

"Yeah, you. Interfering, obstructing justice—the staties won't put up with any of it." Hamson mumbled something about him not putting up with me, either, whatever that was supposed to mean.

"Back to my point. Her handbag was a Louis Vuitton. If this had been a robbery, they would have definitely taken it."

Hamson shook his head and swiped his upper lip before resuming eye contact. "Don't you think I know that? Trust me, I already deduced that much."

"This whole competitive, sarcastic thing isn't a good look for you." Total lie since literally everything was a good look for him, but thankfully Verity wasn't there to call me out.

A cool veneer claimed his expression as he slid back into cop mode. "Did you notice anyone else around before you left or after you came back?"

"No, whoever did it was long gone." My mind reeled back to those horrific moments. "There were a bunch of people on the sidewalk and kids who wanted to get into the ice cream shop, but no one was inside when we came back."

"And was there anyone else there before?"

"No, but you should ask Walter. He was still there when Verity and I left."

Hamson's eyebrows flexed, then he made a few tight scribbles on his notepad. "Interesting."

My stomach cratered, and my heart kicked into overdrive when I realized what Hamson meant.

I'd just implicated Walter in the murder of Ruby Maxwell.

Chapter Five

THE AFTER-HOURS cacophony in the Crumb's kitchen from women gabbing, dishes clanking, and the industrial mixer running could only be halted by Polly. She whistled through her fingers to grab our attention. "Can you guys keep it down? I'm trying to hear the rest of the story. I can't believe you found a body *again*."

"You're telling me." I shook my head in disbelief. "Officer Leon even commented on it."

After the tragedy this afternoon, I'd joined the gang at Crumb's to help decorate cookies for tomorrow's drop-off at the women's shelter. While I wasn't great in the kitchen or anything else even remotely domestic, I could squirt frosting with the best of them. Plus, it gave Verity and me a chance to catch the gang up on the details.

Naomi paused mid-bite, the half-eaten cookie poised at her lips. "It's scary to think there's another murderer on the loose in Beaver Bluff."

"I'm just glad you two are okay." Aunt Lulu switched off the mixer and dusted her hands on her apron. "You did your part by talking to the officers, and now you can let them deal with it."

I glopped dark yellow frosting into the piping bag while I finished telling the story. When finished, I leaned against the counter and sighed. "It's a good thing we got to tell you guys about it before all the rumors and second-hand info started."

Verity eyed Lulu, Polly, and Naomi with a serious expression. "Exactly. You know how people are about *murder*." She stage-whispered the last bit as though the cops were listening in. After the way Hamson interviewed me today, it was distinctly possible.

After a little back and forth, Hamson had dismissed me and brought in Verity while I waited outside the bistro with Pooh Bear. Ella came out and offered me a soda and chatted me up with the sweetest smile and lilt in her voice, which was a complete one-eighty compared to the night I saw her at bingo. Being cute as a button with curly brown hair and dimples, I could see why Hamson had taken to eating there.

Not that I was dwelling on it.

"People did go a little nutty after Bronco turned up dead." Naomi slung the strap of the Have a Crummy Day apron over her head, careful not to muss her puffy hair. "And now Ruby. I just can't fathom something so awful happening in our little town *again*."

"I don't know why you're all so concerned about this. I mean, I get that it's terrible, but it's not like Ruby was a great friend to any of us," Polly said matter-of-factly. "May she rest in peace."

"Oh, here we go again with the phony condolences." Aunt Lulu pinched the bridge of her nose.

"Who says I'm being phony? Just because Ruby was the biggest gossip in town and flaunted her money hither and yon doesn't mean I hope she's *not* resting in peace." Polly grabbed a piping bag and joined me at the counter.

"Be that as it may, my advice is, stay out of it this time." Lulu raised her eyebrows in my general direction.

"I totally agree." I toasted her with a cookie. "Besides, Hamson warned me about that when he interviewed me."

"Why was he doing the interviews, anyway?" Lulu asked.

Verity offered a half-shrug. "When he was talking to me, he

sort of implied there was no other detective in the department available, and things are still a little chaotic."

"That certainly isn't going to help matters." I teased just enough frosting out of the bag to add a curlicue to my design. "Still, I don't want any part of this. I *am* a little concerned about Walter."

Naomi's eyes turned watery, and she pulled a tissue out of her bra. "I just hope he's okay. What an awful thing to happen in his shop. I thought about calling him, but it seemed too forward."

"After the things you did back in the eighties, and you're saying a phone call is forward?" Polly snorted.

"Hey now, that was a long time ago before—"

"Polly, that was a little rude—"

"I can't believe you just said that."

Everyone spoke at once until Verity clapped. "Can we please keep it down?"

"Says the librarian." Naomi giggled, seemingly happier now that the conversation moved off Walter.

Verity grimaced. "Very funny. Anyway, I think Officer Hamson is eyeing Walter since he was the last to see Ruby alive. At least that's what KC told him."

Everyone looked at me, slack-jawed.

Naomi jumped in first. "After such a tragedy happened in his shop, and then you go pointing a finger at him? How could you *do* that?"

I shrank a little inside. "I didn't say it exactly like that. Besides, I'm sure Verity told Hamson the same thing, right?"

She shook her head slowly. "Oh, no. I wouldn't say that because I don't know for absolute certain who was the last to see her alive. I mean, technically, the last person to see her alive would've been the killer."

The volume in the kitchen rose to epic proportions as everyone hammered me for telling Hamson what I knew. What could I have done differently? Walter was the last one in the shop with Ruby, as far as I knew. And how much did I really know about Walter?

I discarded the thought. There was no way the sweet older man could have bumped off Ruby. Although maybe what I saw as Walter being upset—the jittery hands, the sweat on his forehead—was actually his guilty conscience. But what reason would he have to kill her?

"Now you *have* to help him." Naomi's pleading tone stopped the noise.

"No, I don't want my niece involved again. It's too dangerous, and I don't want to hear any arguments about it." Lulu fisted her hands on her hips. "We *all* need to stay out of it. Agreed?"

Everyone grumbled.

I started decorating the next cookie, this time with a bag of orange frosting to make it look like an autumn leaf. "I wouldn't even know where to start, anyway. I don't know anything about Ruby's life or who wanted her out of the picture."

"My money is on the grandson." The certainty in Polly's voice caught my attention.

I set the piping bag aside. "What makes you think it's him?"

Everyone stopped working and leaned in.

"The feeling in my gut, which is rarely wrong. I'll bet it really is about the money." Polly nodded as though agreeing with herself. "Think about it. Ruby was loaded. And just who do you think is set to inherit?"

"Do we know that for a fact?" Verity asked.

"If it's true, then that's a pretty big motive." Naomi ate the rest of her cookie. "She had millions of dollars, and they have to go somewhere."

Lulu hiked an eyebrow. "Money isn't the only thing people kill for, though. Remember on bingo night, she was talking about that marriage she interfered in by telling the wife what her husband was doing? It could easily be something like that, too."

"That's right—it was the man who owns the sporting goods shop, right next door to Walter's." I snapped my fingers. "And

Ruby was strangled by a rope that looked like the kind used by rock climbers." Not that I actually knew the difference between rock climbing rope and other kinds of ropes.

"Wait, wait, wait." Lulu held up her hands. "Let's not get carried away. We need to let the police do their jobs."

I rolled my eyes. "Yeah, we all know how that worked out last time. Anyway, it was probably Ella."

The ladies gasped in unison.

"I mean, c'mon. Is everyone forgetting the blowout they had at bingo?" I glanced around the kitchen. "It's so obvious, *and* her bistro is right next door to Walter's place, too. She could have slipped in there while we were all across the street."

"It's *too* obvious," Polly said. "After that big fight, she'd be foolish to bump off Ruby."

"It makes sense, though." I gave up on decorating and ate the cookie. "That's why she was so helpful with her you-can-use-my-office-for-questioning act."

"She could've also been helpful because she knew people would point the finger at her because of that argument, even if she's innocent." Verity blew the hole in my theory.

Polly leaned against the counter and folded her arms. "You're just jealous because Hamson has been eating at the bistro instead of here."

"No, I'm not." My words came too quickly to sound true. "I'm just floating theories like the rest of you, and mine makes just as much sense. Think about it. Ruby is the supposed reason Ella is going out of business, so there's the motive. And Ella's bistro is right next door to Walter, so there's the opportunity."

"And she just happened to see Ruby, and happened to be carrying a rope, and happened to see an opportunity when there was a random gunshot?" Polly's eyebrows quirked.

"Well, someone had to have done it," Verity said. "It's more likely her than Walter."

"Exactly. Besides, it could never be Walter." Naomi grimaced in my general direction as though I'd actually accused him. "I'll bet his business will take a big hit after this." She paused, then looked at me with much kinder eyes than before. "Hey, maybe you can do some of that social promotional stuff for him, too, like you're doing here. He's going to need it."

I sighed. "You're probably right, but I've been pretty busy with the grand reopening plans. We're less than a week away."

"And don't forget you're helping my friend," Polly said.

"She's coming here tomorrow for a consultation." I ate another cookie. So far, I'd eaten as many as I'd frosted. "After that, I'll head over to Walter's and see if I can talk him into it."

In fact, it would probably be a good chance to scope out Ella's place and see if I could sniff anything out. Her goody-two-shoes act might fool the others, but it definitely didn't fool me.

***

AFTER WE FINISHED DECORATING the cookies, Verity came back to my place for an impromptu self-defense lesson. Not to brag, but I was getting pretty good at elbow strikes and leg sweeps, thanks to my best friend's training.

"Are you sure you don't want to run through the sequence just one more time?" Verity readjusted the floor mat she'd purchased to use at my place. It clashed with the contemporary chic furniture I'd purchased at an estate sale—furniture that was decidedly better than the garish décor left in the house by the rental agency when I'd moved in.

"I think I'm done for the night. Besides, Pooh Bear needs a walk before bedtime." At the sound of his name, my trusty canine's ears perked. He strutted over to his toy box and plucked out his leash. Smartypants.

My phone buzzed on the coffee table we'd pushed to the wall. I reached for it and pressed the button. A jolt of adrenaline zinged through my veins, and my brain tripped over itself to make sense of what I saw.

"What is it?" Verity leaned over to see.

"A text message from my ex, James Carlisle." I bit my lip, unsure what to do.

Verity grabbed the phone and opened the message. "Good grief—loser."

"What's it say?" I couldn't bring myself to read it.

"That he's really missing you, and you guys should talk." She tapped the faceplate. "Delete, delete, delete."

"Was there more?"

She shook her head. "You don't want to know."

"You're right." Actually, she was so wrong, but I didn't want to admit it. Even though I'd heard from a few friends back in LA, I hadn't expected to hear from him.

"Let's go. Pooh Bear's ready." She tugged me out the door. "Besides, we have more important things to discuss, if you know what I mean."

There was nothing like a little murder to take your mind off a broken heart.

The three of us started walking around my dimly lit neighborhood that bordered the forest. After finding a dead body in my garage when I first came to town, I didn't think I'd ever be able to settle in. But after I got Pooh Bear for protection and we solved the murder, I'd come to enjoy my little corner of Beaver Bluff. I'd even started getting to know some neighbors, in addition to Krystal from Crumb's and her husband Clyde, who lived across the street.

"So…what do you think really happened to Ruby?" I picked up the pace as Pooh Bear led the way down Moss Grove Lane. A chill closed in, and the smell of wood smoke wafted through the air. It was probably time to put away my heeled sandals and trade them in for sturdy shoes like everyone else wore, but I wasn't quite ready to make that move.

Verity zipped up her jacket. "Like I said to the gang— someone had to do it. And it had to be a crime of opportunity since no one could know that the shop would clear out because of a gunshot across the street."

"You're right. No one could've known there wouldn't be anyone else there." Unless it was Walter.

No, it couldn't have been him. Walter was our friend and an upstanding member of the community. He was a bingo caller, for goodness' sake. I needed to stop letting my overactive imagination lead me astray.

I casually glanced up at my friend. "You know we can't just stay out of it, right?"

Verity clapped. "I was waiting for you to say that. So, what's the plan?"

"I've been trying to come up with one." My heels clacked against the sidewalk, echoing against the quiet of the night. "Tomorrow, after I finish up at Crumb's, we should start by going back to the scene."

"Do you think the police will have released it by then?"

I shrugged. "Who knows? But we can at least check, plus I promised to talk to Walter. Then it wouldn't hurt to ask Ella a few questions, like where she was when the gunshot went off."

Verity stopped me. "You know your aunt is going to kill us if she finds out."

"Yeah. I think this time it's going to be harder all the way around."

Between Naomi being Team Walter, Polly being Team Ella, and Lulu being Team Stay-Out-Of-It, we definitely had our share of obstacles. And if Verity and I somehow found the murderer, would we lose a friend?

Chapter Six

I FELT sorry for Polly's young friend for a few reasons, not the least of which was having a name like Trudi Bucket. Add to that the fact she only had three faithful followers on social media—Erman, Mary, and Tom—and my heartstrings were plucked. Finally, here was someone I could help.

"Can I get you another cup of coffee while we finish up?" I closed my notebook and exited her social media accounts. "It's freshly brewed all day long. I could even fix you up with a pastry." Though it was busy inside Crumb's, I wasn't above plying my first paying client with free baked goods.

She reached for her satchel. "No, thank you. I really should get going. The groomer is coming in half an hour to get a few of our newest additions ready to post on social media."

By additions, I assumed she meant stray animals she took in at her small farm that doubled as an animal shelter just south of town. Unfortunately, I didn't think three likes on their posts would be much help for the homeless pets. Hopefully, I could fix her accounts sooner rather than later, for their sake.

I switched off my tablet. "I'll just send you my notes, along with a few ideas I have for graphics to get you started. Once you're set-up, we can flesh out ideas for the adopt-a-pet day."

"I'm so glad to have help. The only thing I know about social media is that your posts get buried if no one likes them right away." Trudi stood and slung the strap of her purse over her shoulder. "I really hope this works, if not with adoptions, at least with more people supporting the cause."

There went my heartstrings again. Or maybe my heart was still jumbled from last night's text from James. I hadn't responded, thankfully, but that didn't mean I'd forgotten about it. I tried to imagine why he would bother contacting me more than a month after I'd left LA but couldn't come up with a good reason. Just as well, since I had no intention of talking to him again.

"Don't worry. We're going to increase your exposure and start finding homes for your furry family." I patted her arm. "I should probably get going, too. I need to help our friend after what happened yesterday. Can you believe there was another murder here in Beaver Bluff?"

Trudi gasped. "That's awful. I hadn't heard."

"I'm surprised. Ruby Maxwell is all anyone is talking about."

"Ruby?" Her voice softened. "I know Ruby. She's one of our monthly donors." Her forehead wrinkled, and her lips parted as though she had more to say but didn't know what.

"Oh, no. I'm so sorry." I prayed she didn't start to cry. Why hadn't I been more sensitive? It never occurred to me that someone would be upset.

"What happened to her?"

The last thing I wanted to do was give Trudi a blow-by-blow of Ruby's death. Instead, I stuffed my tablet into my handbag. "I…there was…." I glanced around Crumb's, my gaze going everywhere but towards her. "I don't know all the details." An imaginary Verity scolded me inside my head for not telling the absolute truth, although it was true that I didn't know *all* the details, like who actually killed Ruby.

"I have to go." Trudi offered a sad smile then pivoted toward the door, nearly bumping into Polly and Naomi. They were just coming in after securing Pooh Bear's leash to the bench out front.

"We'll find a way to help your animals," I called after her as she left, causing a few customers to look my way.

Polly exchanged a brief greeting with Trudi, then wandered to my table. "What on earth happened?"

"Guess I pretty much made sure that I lost my first real client." I bit my lip. "I mentioned Ruby's murder without realizing that she knew her."

"Good going." Polly rolled her eyes.

"Speaking of murder," Naomi said as she pulled out a chair, "have you been to see Walter yet?"

"I was waiting until Verity came so we could go together. She should be having her lunch break soon, and she wanted to grab a snack here first." I glanced at the cat clock on the wall, its tail swinging toward noon.

"You'll have to come back and tell us all everything that Walter says. Tell us how he's feeling and if he's holding up okay." Naomi pleaded with her eyes.

"But that's *all* you'd better be talking about." Aunt Lulu flipped a Have a Crummy Day towel over her shoulder. "Remember what we discussed last night."

I resisted the urge to cross my fingers behind my back and lie and instead settled for a noncommittal grunt. "We all agreed that I need to offer Walter some help, just in case his business is taking a hit. For all I know, the police haven't even allowed him to reopen the shop yet."

Naomi glanced around to make sure the customers weren't listening. "The least you can do is try, after pointing the officers in his direction."

"That's not what happened." I stood as Verity strolled into Crumb's. "All I said was that they should ask him if there was anyone else in the shop with Ruby when he left." At least, I thought that was how it went down. This wasn't like a crime show where everyone remembered exactly what they said and when they said it.

"We trust you." Naomi squeezed my hand. "You'll figure out what happened."

"No, she won't," Lulu argued.

I walked away as the gang continued to bicker about what I was and wasn't allowed to do. Verity flashed me a questioning look as I approached. I shook my head. "Trust me, you don't want to know."

IF THE YELLOW crime scene tape wasn't enough to ward us off, the officer standing at the front door of Yum Yum's did the trick.

"How long before you guys are done in here?" I glanced at the tiny gold name badge while trying to keep Pooh Bear from getting too close. "Officer Kirby."

His stoic expression revealed nothing, especially behind dark sunglasses. "It takes as long as it takes."

"It's just that we…." I glanced at Verity. "Need ice cream." Definitely true.

"I'm sure you can find some elsewhere." Not even a hint of a smile tipped his mouth.

Verity pulled a card from her pocket. "Can you give us a call when you're finished?"

Officer Kirby didn't reach for it. "You can come back and find out like everyone else."

I glanced past him, where I could see a sliver of the action between the blinds. Officers—or maybe they were crime scene techs or the state police Hamson had threatened me with—poked around inside. A big change from the last murder, for sure.

"All right, we'll come back." I edged away from the officer and turned to Verity, shielding my eyes from the noonday sun. "Let's go inside the sporting goods shop."

"Why?"

I gritted my teeth and nodded towards the store. "To see what they have to *offer*." Apparently, Verity didn't remember our discussion about Ruby having told me the trouble she'd caused between the owner and his soon-to-be-ex-wife.

Suddenly, Verity waved enthusiastically. "Look, there's Walter."

Walter sat on a park bench across the street under the shade of an oak, staring vacantly at his shop. At the sight of Verity, his despondent expression turned to joy. He motioned for us to come over.

"You go ahead." I glanced at the sporting goods shop. "I'm just going to run in there and use the ladies' room. I'll be back in a minute." I handed Pooh Bear's leash to her, and he offered one of his soft barks to acknowledge our parting.

Verity and Pooh trotted across the road while I ducked inside A Good Sport. It took a moment for my eyes to adjust to the dim light. The inside appeared much larger than the storefront suggested, perhaps three or four times the size of Walter's shop. The teenaged boy at the square cash wrap near the entrance offered a lazy greeting, allowing me to slip past him and peruse the aisles unnoticed.

Sportswear, camping goods, and even kayaks filled the shop. They had everything but customers. If I could find the owner, maybe I could sneak in a few questions, like where he'd been when the gunshot incident happened yesterday. The problem was, I had no idea what the owner looked like.

The back wall held what appeared to be gear for rock climbing. Not that I knew for certain that's what I was seeing. Clamps, clips…and rope. Blue rope, not unlike the one that dangled from Ruby's neck just yesterday. I edged closer to the gear, noting the packaging on the rope, which obviously hadn't been on the one I'd seen yesterday.

"Can I help you find anything?"

I startled and clutched my chest at the sight of the teenaged boy who had appeared out of nowhere. "I didn't see you…I…" *was looking for a possible murder weapon.* "I need the restroom."

He swept the hair out of his face, then motioned to a hall at the very back of the store. "It's that way." He watched me, curiosity lingering in his eyes. "Through the hallway," he said, apparently waiting for me to go right now.

"Great, I'll just…." I scooted around him and hustled to the hallway, hoping he'd leave so I could go back and examine the ropes more closely without an audience. Maybe the owner really had a bone to pick with Ruby and seized the opportunity to bump her off when everyone else ran across the street. He happened to have a rope, and things got out of hand.

It sounded implausible, even to me. But the point remained, *someone* had to have killed Ruby, and the owner of this shop would have had the opportunity—and the rope.

Ideas swam in my head as I pushed through the back door and ended up in a dark hallway running perpendicular to the one I'd just exited. Apparently, I'd missed the bathroom and ended up —I glanced around to orient myself—in another hall, not an alley. It appeared to run the length of the strip mall, connecting the stores to one another.

Interesting.

To my right would be Walter's shop, as evidenced by the crime scene tape cordoning off the door—a door that was propped open. Voices floated into the hallway, echoing off the cinderblock walls.

Slowly, I tiptoed closer, careful not to let my heels clack against the concrete floor. Four more steps, three, two. I paused outside the door and listened. Considering the angle, the sound would travel better if I stood on the other side.

I held my breath and scurried to the other side of the open door, closer to the backside of the bistro. Through the crack in the door, I spied Hamson and Officer Leon, along with two others who had state police logos emblazoned on their polo shirts, just out front of the small stockroom.

"Where was her grandson during the whole thing?" One of the officers fisted his hands on his waist, taking the stance of someone used to being in charge. He was definitely a level up from our small Beaver Bluff crew. "During the debrief, someone mentioned they were together almost all the time like he was her caretaker."

"David was nowhere near here, at least that we could tell." The ugly police uniform did nothing to detract from Officer Leon's natural beauty. Some women had all the luck.

Officer Kirby appeared, apparently no longer guarding the front door. "If we can find evidence of him being here, that might be our guy."

The other officer, an older man with a deep scowl and gruff voice, spoke. "No, we follow the evidence to form a theory, not the other way around. That said, we still need to talk to him and establish an alibi."

Good idea. Maybe I could get to him first—not that I was trying to interfere. I simply didn't trust the Beaver Bluff PD, and with good reason, judging by how the outsider had to tell our local officers to work out the evidence before forming theories. Although, to be fair, the gang and I had basically been doing the same thing.

"Hopefully, we'll finish up here before long," Hamson said. "Let's go out back to take a breather."

"Good idea," the officer in charge said with a curt tone. "Hopefully, none of those busybodies are out there. You'd better believe I'll take care of them real quick."

Oh no.

I glanced around for a way of escape.

If I crossed over the door back towards the sporting goods store, Hamson and the others would see me, and if I went out the door that appeared to lead to the alley, he and whoever came with him would see me there too. After the way he'd warned me to steer clear of the investigation and told me what the staties would do, I could *not* let anyone find out I'd been listening in.

There was only one way to go—towards the bistro.

My heels made a shuffling sound as I hustled down the hallway. Only a few steps to go, and I could already taste the freedom.

Unless Ella or one of her staff caught me. But better her than the police. I'd make up an excuse. I got lost, I was looking for the bathroom (partially true), I was…

I pushed through the bistro's back door and ended up…in the same windowless, closet-like room where I'd been questioned yesterday. The only light came from a computer screen on the desktop. If I could just hide long enough for the officers to go outside, I could cross back into the sporting goods shop.

Footsteps echoed in the hallway, approaching the bistro instead of heading into the alley.

Had they heard me? Surely, they couldn't have moved that fast.

Still, the steps came closer. Did I dare run into the front of the bistro and risk having to explain myself to Ella?

I glanced around for an answer. The desk. The underside was small, but it was the only chance I had. Quickly, I dove under the desk and tucked myself in like a turtle, my knees scrunched to my chest and my heels poking my bottom.

The blood hammering through my veins drowned out the sound of the footsteps, and I fought to hold my breath as the door creaked open.

Chapter Seven

THE SOUND of shoes against linoleum filled the tiny space as the officer took a step, then paused, then stepped again.

Maybe they'd go away, and I could sneak out, unnoticed.

A cramp worked its way up my leg, and I forced myself to remain still. Just a few more moments until the person gave up and I could go home. Never set foot at a crime scene again. It was a good time to start minding my own business.

A bead of sweat slid off my forehead and dropped to the floor just as dark shoes appeared in my vision.

I gulped, willing the officer to leave.

Suddenly, Hamson leaned down and met my eye. "Just as I thought. Are you looking for something?"

I squeaked and willed my thumping heart to dial it down a notch. "Oh, good. It's just you." I shimmied out from under the desk.

"What do you mean, 'it's just you?'" Despite the irritation in Hamson's voice, he thrust his hand toward me, and I reluctantly accepted. He pulled me to my feet as though I weighed nothing, despite all the scones and raspberry tarts I'd been scarfing down for the past month.

"I mean, oh good, it's you, my pal from Crumb's."

Hamson leaned dangerously close, his dark gaze holding me captive. "Pal?"

"Friend?"

He shook his head.

"Customer?" I released his hand and dusted off my sundress. "Never mind. The point is, I'm glad it was you."

"Because…" His eyebrow quirked.

"How did you see me, anyway?" I asked, ignoring his prompt.

"You're the only person I know who would wear a bright orange dress and think she wouldn't be noticed standing at the back door of a crime scene." Hamson's quiet voice sent shivers down my spine. He was a tough nut to crack, but I wasn't going to let that stop me.

"Oh, you saw me there?" I asked meekly.

Hamson nodded, a ghost of a smile on his soft lips. "And the same dress was sticking out from under the desk just now."

"Brilliant detective work," I teased. "Bravo."

Laughter sounded outside the office door that led to the bistro. Hamson's gaze darted around the tiny office. He sent a warning look as he whisked open the back door, grabbed my hand, and flung me into the hallway. With brisk steps, he toted me back toward the sporting goods shop.

He stopped and released my hand, but his dark eyes lingered. "If anyone asks, you were lost. I was helping you find your way."

"You want me to lie," I whispered, noting the way my fingers still tingled from his touch. "I'm not that kind of person." *Mostly*.

Hamson's face hardened. "Well, it's your neck."

"Why, officer, are you saying that you're concerned about me?" I cringed at my flirty tone, but that didn't stop me from continuing. "I knew it."

He sighed, then threw a glance over his shoulder. "Look, I just don't want any complications, that's *all*."

Based on the way he'd grabbed my hand, I wanted to challenge his statement. But I wanted answers about the murder investigation more. "So…you and Officer Leon don't think it's David, either."

"How much did you overhear? And no one ever said that."

"So, you *do* think it may have been David." I pondered the likelihood of Ruby's grandson being involved, and it seemed possible. After all, he probably had the most to gain, at least financially.

"I didn't say that, either." He gripped his gun belt. "Has anything I've said sunk into your head? Anything at all?" His incredulous expression was annoyingly endearing.

"Of course." *Not.* "I'm not trying to get involved. It's just that we're worried about Walter and what this is doing to his business."

Hamson's mouth tightened as though he'd stopped himself from revealing something.

"What is it? What were you about to say?" I prodded.

"Never mind. We're all working as best we can, and the staties want to get this finished and go home. Believe me, everyone is working around the clock to nab the killer."

"So, they're trying to rush this along?"

"Don't put words in my mouth." His expression hardened. "And while you're worried about your friend, we're looking at the bigger picture. There's more to it than you realize."

"Wait, do you actually think Walter could have done it? Because I can tell you—" I looked around to ensure our privacy. "He's *not* responsible for what happened to Ruby. I know I may have implied that he was the last one to see her alive, but I didn't mean it like *that.* You should know better than to pick on a sweet old man."

"No one is picking on anyone. This is police work, and it would take more than a comment from you—"

"Hey—"

"As reliable as you are, to place someone under suspicion."

"So, you're saying you have more intel on *Walter?*" At the sound of a door opening at the other end of the hallway, I craned my neck to see around Hamson. Someone from the bistro was hauling out a few trash bags, paying no attention to us.

"I didn't say that." He shook his head, his police-y expression back in full force. "I don't even know why I'm discussing this with you."

Our gazes connected, and my breath hitched. I inched closer and smiled. "Oh, I think you know exactly why you're talking to me, and why you pulled me out of the bistro, and why you—"

"It's not what you think it is." The glint in his eye said otherwise. Hamson did a slow pivot and left me in front of the restrooms that I'd completely overlooked earlier. His words replayed in my head, the softness of his tone and the shape of his mouth when he spoke. He could recite the Gettysburg Address and cause women everywhere to swoon.

Verity poked her head out of the sporting goods store. "Oh, there you are."

Slowly, everything in the dingy hallway came back into focus, as though I'd been in some kind of stupor while talking to him. Would I ever learn the fine art of playing hard to get? I made my way toward my friend. "I think Hamson just gave me another clue, but I really don't know what to make of it…or of him."

"Don't make anything of him. Officer Hamson is off-limits, remember? If he was into you, he wouldn't keep you guessing." She ushered me back inside the sporting goods shop.

"But sometimes, the way we connect, it's like…"

"I think the connection"—she air-quoted with her fingers—"is one-sided. Now, tell me about the clue." She looped her arm through mine and leaned close.

Casually, we strolled past the teenaged clerk. I looked around one last time to see if we could spot someone who looked like an owner before we walked out the door and into the sunshine. "I overheard the officers talking, and it reminded me that we should find David and see where he was and what he knows before the cops talk to him again." I took a deep breath and carefully weighed my words. "And then we need to take a closer look at Walter."

"THAT'S IT—YOU'VE lost your marbles." Verity scratched Pooh Bear behind the ears before she ushered him into the front seat of my car. We'd both given up on trying to get him to ride anything but shotgun.

We'd decided to stop at my house to drop off Pooh Bear before we hunted for more clues. Then with a whine and a wrinkly forehead, he talked us into taking him along. Despite being a killer canine who'd saved my bacon last month, he was a loveable pooch, and I had a terrible time saying no.

"Thank you for caring about my marbles, but I'm telling you when Walter's name came up, Hamson implied there was more to the story." I walked around to the driver's side and climbed in while Verity slid into the backseat.

"This is Walter we're talking about. There's no way he could be guilty. What would he have against Ruby, anyway?"

"That's what we need to find out." I reached for a dog treat inside my handbag and handed it to Pooh Bear. "Think about it. We can't rule anyone out just because we know and like them. We have to look at all the evidence and then form our theories." I echoed what I'd overheard the cops say.

"We don't *have* evidence."

I turned on the car and revved the engine. "We will after we do a little investigating."

"Your aunt is going to kill you."

"What she doesn't know won't kill me." I slid my sunglasses on. "Let's go see David."

"Do you even have his address?"

"No, but you're a librarian, aren't you?" I flicked my hand at her. "Do your library thing and find him."

"Fine, but we can't just show up at his house. That would be rude."

I backed out of the driveway. "At a time like this, people

expect others to drop by and offer condolences. It's the only decent thing to do."

Verity sat back and buckled her seatbelt. "Not without food."

And that's how we ended up at the deli inside the grocery store one street over from the town square. Shoppers milled about, wheeling carts up and down the crowded aisles while a cheesy selection of music from yesteryear played overhead.

"Literally anything would be better than potato salad." Verity pointed to the giant tub in my arms.

"It's quick and easy, and then we won't have to wait in line for the hot stuff." A shopper jostled me from behind. "The whole idea is to get in, get out, and head to David's."

A tap on my tub startled me.

"This isn't going to help with your workouts." Griff, my some-times-personal trainer, shook his head with disappointment.

I glanced at the arm basket he carried, filled with leafy greens and protein drinks. "What, this? It's not for me."

"It's been a while since I've seen you at the gym. There's an opening in my schedule for tomorrow morning." His arms flexed as he adjusted his basket. "I'll help you get back on track."

"I'd love to do that, but with the grand reopening of Crumb's this weekend, I'm super busy."

"Six a.m., sharp. It's a great way to kick-start your day."

I issued a non-committal mumble that might not have been very nice before switching subjects. "You and Holly will be at the reopening, won't you? There'll be food and prizes and contests—"

"Only if there's some healthy snacks for me and Holly. We're trying to get in shape before the wedding." He glanced at his biceps. Even his muscles had muscles.

"Definitely healthy snacks." I made a mental note to add that to accommodate Griff and Holly, the rental agent for my house that I'd had a few run-ins with when I first came to town.

"Tomorrow, six." He tapped my tub again before he walked away.

"Let's go." I tugged Verity toward the check-out lines that

snaked out three or four people deep. Briefly, I considered swapping out the potato salad for wings and wedge fries, but with so much to do, time was critical. It'd be fine.

We hooked onto the shortest line and perused the magazine headlines while we waited. Moments later, another person queued behind us, quietly chatting on her phone.

"I got the herbs. They're terrible here, but it's not like it matters now, thanks to the stupid old crone." The terse voice sounded familiar.

Out of the corner of my eye, I saw the brown curls first. I nudged Verity and flung a glance over my shoulder at Ella. The bistro owner continued her rant, more in line with how she'd acted at bingo than how she'd been so "helpful" after the murder yesterday.

Then it hit me…what if she'd seen me escaping her office? My pulse kicked up a notch. But, wait, if she had, she would have come after Hamson and me in the hallway. I let out a slow breath while I leaned backward to hear her conversation.

Unfortunately, she hung up.

I turned. "Everything okay?"

"You sound a little upset," Verity chimed in.

"Oh, it's you two." Ella reached for the charm on her necklace and zipped it back and forth. "Sorry. I'm having a bad couple of days."

"Not as bad as some people." I edged closer. "Like Ruby." A.k.a. the stupid old crone—the one who had driven the bistro out of business.

Ella patted her chest as her eyes rounded. "That was simply awful. I still haven't gotten over the shock."

Verity tilted her head, her lie-dar going off. "Did you know her?"

Ella hesitated. "Not well, no."

"Still, in a town this size, a *murder* affects everyone, especially since it happened right next door to you, and after that fight, you two had an argument at bingo." I scrutinized her face for telltale signs.

Ella choked. "Oh, that was just a little squabble. It's no secret we weren't friends. Still, I couldn't believe everything that happened yesterday."

"We were close by, too. When the gunshot went off, we ran across the street." I watched her closely. "I don't remember seeing you there."

"Gunshot?" Ella's gaze volleyed between us. "I vaguely remember hearing about that. I wasn't at the bistro when it happened."

Probably because she was next door murdering Ruby.

"Too bad you missed all the action." Verity moved forward in line and pulled a pack of gum off the rack. "Where were you, exactly?"

A flash of irritation crossed Ella's face before she regained her smooth veneer. "Here, I think. I keep running out of things, and I'm not placing any big orders before I close." Her voice warbled on the last word.

"You *think* you were here?" I adjusted the tub in my arms.

Ella's eyes narrowed. "What difference does it make? Anyway, when I got back, I offered Officer Hamson the use of my office." Her mouth slid into an easy smile. "He was more than happy for my help."

My fingers clenched the tub. "I'm sure he was since your office is quite cozy." And full of dust bunnies. Flashbacks of my time tucked under her desk filled my head. Maybe Ruby was right in reporting the bistro to the health department.

"That's a lot of potato salad," Ella said, switching subjects.

I angled the tub away from her. "It's for Ruby's grandson. We were heading over to offer our condolences."

Ella frowned. "Interesting choice."

"Everyone likes potato salad."

"I make a killer potato salad. You should stop by sometime." Ella's dimples deepened when she smirked.

"I'll just do that." I turned away.

What was so fantastic about Ella? She even had Polly snook-ered, and Polly never fell for anything. And Officer Hamson, too. Apparently, Verity and I were the only ones who saw through her whole innocent routine.

After her comments on my choice of condolence food, I was more determined than ever to figure out where Ella really was when Ruby bit the dust.

Chapter Eight

THE FACT that David lived with Ruby came as no surprise. Neither was the fact their palatial house overlooked the ocean and had a gated entrance. Lucky for us, the gate was open when we pulled into the gravel driveway.

"What are we actually looking for here today?" Verity unbuckled her seatbelt.

"Anything suspicious, out of place, or just doesn't seem right." I applied a coat of gloss and smacked my lips in the rearview mirror. "Think about it. This guy probably stands to inherit millions now that his grandma is out of the picture."

"But they did everything together, and he already lived here. He likely had access to the millions without her being 'out of the picture.'"

"True, but we still have to establish where he was at the time of the murder. From what I overheard, the police haven't really verified his whereabouts even after talking to him."

Verity frowned. "It seems like we're intruding on his grief."

"We're not intruding. We're offering condolences. I'm as anxious as you are to get this all behind us so I can focus on the grand reopening of Crumb's and building up a little business for myself here in Beaver Bluff. The sooner we figure out what really happened to Ruby, the sooner we can all move on."

She drew a deep breath. "True. I just don't feel right being here under false pretenses."

"Are you going to tell him how sorry you are about his grandma?"

"Yes."

"Then there's nothing false about it. Besides, we're trying to figure out who killed his grandma, so we're actually doing them a favor. Now let's get to it." I grabbed my tub of potato salad, and before I could shut the door to my car, Pooh Bear hopped out after me, his leash in his mouth. "Oh, fine, you big mutt." I clipped the leash to his collar, then he trotted up the brick walkway ahead of us and sat on the wide porch.

The doorbell gonged, the sound reverberating through the house.

"Remember, look for anything at all that seems suspicious," I whispered seconds before the ten-foot-tall door swung open.

David, his dark hair disheveled, stood before us wearing sweats and a stained t-shirt. He looked completely different than the well put together man we'd met previously. He even wore black-rimmed glasses that were slightly askew. "Can I help you?"

Pooh Bear barked. David jumped back, his eyes rounding in surprise.

"Naughty." I tapped my dog's nose. "Sorry about that. Do you remember me from Crumb's?"

"That's right, you're KC." His expression softened as he looked up at Verity, who stood a few inches taller than him. "And who might this be?"

"I'm Verity. I saw you at bingo the other night, but we weren't introduced." She proffered her hand, which he clasped longer than necessary.

"Verity…the name suits you."

"Why, thank you." She smiled coyly.

I cleared my throat to remind them I was standing there, too. "May we come in?"

David glanced down, his nose curling slightly at my panting dog. "Only if you leave him outside."

"Happy to." I tied his leash loosely around a ceramic flower-pot, so if he happened to get loose, he wouldn't take the flowers with him.

The inside of the house appeared even larger than the outside, with the cavernous foyer at least two stories high. Our shoes echoed on the tile floor as David led us past a curving staircase to a library with floor-to-ceiling bookcases on three sides. The fourth side was a wall of windows overlooking the ocean, with an old-fashioned desk posi-tioned nearby. Rather than inviting us to sit, we stood in the center of the room near the pristine furniture arranged in a semicircle.

"I'm afraid you caught me at a bad time." David patted his chest as though trying to compose his emotions. "Going through Gran's things is harder than I thought it would be."

Verity reached out and cupped his upper arm. "We're so sorry for your loss."

"Absolutely. We know at a time like this, it's easy to forget to take care of yourself, so we brought you this." I held out the tub.

David took it with hesitation and scanned the label. "Potato salad. Thank you." His statement of gratitude sounded more like a question. "I'll just go put this away." He excused himself and left the room.

"Quick, look around," I whispered.

Verity craned her neck every which way. It didn't help that we had no idea what we should look for. I scurried to the desk to see what David might have been working on before we arrived.

An appointment book opened to today sat in the middle of the desk. Three meetings were inked in, then crossed through with the word "canceled" written next to each one. Was David also Ruby's private secretary, or was this just one of the tasks left to her survivor?

I whipped out my phone and snapped a picture, just in case something here mattered.

"He's coming." Verity's loud stage whisper startled me. Apparently, the kitchen was closer than I'd imagined.

I hustled away from the desk and pretended to admire the view from the window. Not that it needed pretending. "Would you get a load of this? Breathtaking." The sun would soon touch the ocean with an explosion of color. I saw David approach in the window's reflection.

"Gran loved to sit here on evenings like this with her tea." His mournful voice made me a little sad for him, although maybe it was a little *too* mournful to be genuine.

"It must have come as quite a shock to you." I spun to face him. "It was certainly shocking for us. We'd seen her shortly before…."

He covered his mouth. "Indeed. If only I'd been with her, then maybe this wouldn't have happened."

Verity was instantly at his side, patting his back gently. "You can't blame yourself."

"You certainly can't." *Unless you did it.* "Were you supposed to have been with her yesterday at that time?" I leaned against the arm of the couch and hoped David would invite us to have a seat.

He didn't.

"Usually, I accompanied Gran on her daily outings, but yesterday I scheduled a haircut. I was going to meet her afterward." David smoothed his tousled locks with his hand—locks that didn't appear any shorter than the last time I'd seen him. "She was planning on meeting someone else, anyway, so I didn't think she needed me."

"You were such a good grandson to Ruby." Verity clasped her hands. "I'm sure she appreciated you very much."

David gazed at Verity, his sad expression lifting. "Yes, I believe she did."

Did she appreciate him to the tune of millions? Exactly how much did he stand to inherit? Grandson or not, she appeared to be as hard on David as she was on everyone. Why else would he devote his life to Ruby if not for a big payout at the end? Not that I was cynical.

Okay, maybe a little.

"Do you have any ideas about who could have done it?" I clutched my chest, trying to appear equally distraught. But, to be fair, I was a much better actress before meeting Verity, who insisted on honesty at all times.

David poised his finger by his mouth and shook his head. "I really don't. You might not know this, but she tended to ruffle some feathers from time to time. Still, she was a wonderful, giving person."

Now he was laying it on thick. Not that I wanted to think ill of the dead, but still.

"Do you know who she was supposed to—"

A loud series of barks sounded out front.

"Hurry, I think your dog…" David's voice trailed off as he quickstepped out of the library.

Verity and I followed as the barking continued. When we arrived in the foyer, I saw Pooh Bear through the window. The rascal had gotten loose and was chasing after a uniform-clad figure.

"Oh, it's the gardener." David pointed at the person circling back around.

"I guess we'd better get going." I rushed to the door, hoping Pooh Bear didn't bite. The last thing I needed right now was a lawsuit from an angry gardener. I swung open the massive door. "Pooh Bear—down!"

Verity hurried past me and caught Pooh's leash. "So sorry. I'm pretty sure he won't bite." She wrangled my dog away from the tow-headed man.

The gardener's expression was a mixture of fear and anger. He picked up his rake and started coming towards us. "Are you crazy or something, lady? Why I ought to—"

"He's mine." I ushered Pooh Bear toward the car. "Won't

happen again." I opened the door and made my dog get inside before the gardener got more upset. I called over my shoulder to David. "We're sorry for your loss!"

Verity barely climbed in and shut the door before I revved the engine and took off.

"Well, that was a bust." Verity buckled her seatbelt as we pulled onto the road.

"Not necessarily." I thought back to our talk, irritated that Pooh Bear cut it short. "I'm more suspicious of David now than I was before."

"What? No." Verity shook her head vehemently. "Didn't you see how upset he was?"

"He was hamming it up. Don't you think it was a little convenient that the one time he's supposedly not at her side, Ruby is murdered?"

"He was getting his hair cut."

"Or was he?" I caught her eye in the rearview mirror. "It looked pretty much the same as it did before, don't you think?"

"Not everyone is lying about everything. Besides, I think his hair looked pretty good for a man in mourning."

Oh, brother.

Naomi was Team Walter, Polly was Team Ella, and now it appeared that Verity was Team David. *Someone* had to be guilty of Ruby's murder, and I was more determined than ever to find out who.

WITH THE SUN sinking low on the horizon and the crisp air chilling me through my light jacket, I decided against working on the front porch when I got home and opted for the kitchen table. Pooh Bear sat at my feet and feigned innocence, as though he hadn't just busted up an important suspect interview.

What had we actually learned today, and what was simply my

suspicions? So much had happened that it was getting hard to keep track, and here it was only the day after the murder.

After heating a frozen dinner designed to satiate someone the size of a toddler, I pulled out my tablet to make notes. Several reminders popped up, mostly to-dos for the grand reopening and notes on appointments with potential clients, one of whom I needed to meet with first thing in the morning. What I really needed was a clear schedule and more time to investigate.

Too bad Verity had to go home early, otherwise, we could've ordered a pizza and started a crime board. The one she made after Bronco Peters was murdered in my garage still sat near the infamous death spot, just a few feet from the kitchen. Thankfully, I'd transformed most of the rental house with furniture I picked up at an estate sale one town over, so the death spot no longer freaked me out.

Even though I loved Beaver Bluff, I wasn't quite ready to make the full investment by pulling all my belongings out of storage in LA. and shipping them up here. There were still opportunities to be had back in California. Just because life knocked me off my high horse didn't mean I had to stay on the ground. Still, the rental was starting to feel a little like home.

I took a bite of ravioli while contemplating our next move. There had to be a way to find out if David had, indeed, been getting his hair cut at the time of Ruby's murder. Likewise, some kind of evidence must exist that Ella was at the grocery store and not sneaking down the back hall into Yum Yum's and killing her nemesis. Also, I still hadn't found the sporting goods shop owner to get a bead on him, even though his shop was right next door and sold the kind of rope Ruby was killed with.

Pooh Bear stood at the back door and whined.

"Need to go out, big guy?"

He nosed the glass.

"I'm coming." My bones creaked, reminding me I had an early morning appointment at the gym with Griff.

I slid open the glass door, and Pooh Bear bounded outside,

frolicking in the evening light. A cool breeze blew in off the ocean that wasn't far from my rental. While the pace of life was definitely slower than LA., it certainly wasn't less eventful.

My phone buzzed with an incoming text. A familiar name popped up, almost as though he'd sensed my nostalgic moment from a thousand miles away.

James Carlisle.

If I were a stronger person, I'd delete it without looking. I always thought I'd be that strong—I *wanted* to be that strong. But no. Deep down, I was still a wuss at heart.

Cautiously, I opened the text.

Gave you time to cool off. Total misunderstanding! When are you coming back? Xoxo.

I jabbed delete with my finger and turned off the phone. Misunderstanding—right. Like I was stupid enough to buy that. Although, in his defense, I occasionally flew off the handle before having all the facts. Was this one of those times?

No.

There was no going back. This was my new life, at least for now, and I was happy with it. Really, Beaver Bluff would be the idyllic place to live out the rest of my days, if only this murder stuff would quit happening.

Chapter Nine

IF THERE WAS a reward for dragging myself to the gym at dawn, I had yet to see it. All I got was a pulled muscle after the eight millionth squat and a lecture from Griff on healthy eating, which didn't stop me from pounding down two squares of coffee cake when I arrived at Crumb's.

I settled myself at a table by the window and took a few moments to gather my thoughts. The smell of fresh bread and the burble of the espresso machine was a balm to my soul. Then an unexpected prospective client came by, referred to me by Verity. I was grateful for the business if a little rushed before my actual scheduled appointment came in.

The woman's name was Melody, and she appeared to be about my age. We spent some time getting to know each other. She told me all the ins and outs of her business before telling me about the festival she needed help promoting. In turn, I explained to her what kind of marketing I specialized in and the preliminary work we needed to do. By the end of our meeting, some good ideas were taking shape.

"I'm glad you stopped by, Melody. It looks like we can implement a few simple strategies for your yarn shop and gain more exposure." I finished making notes on my tablet, excited about the possibility of boosting her fall fiber event.

"I really need this to be a success." Melody leaned close, clad in a knitted sweater, knitted cuffs, and a knitted blue scarf that complemented her bright red hair. "Business has been a little rough lately."

"Sorry to hear that. Have you pinpointed the problem? Does it usually slow down this time of year?"

Melody shook her head. "No, in fact, the change in weather is when people really start to think about bigger knit and crochet projects." She sighed—the deep kind that comes from the soul. "Things haven't been the same since my husband and I started the divorce process. It's been really hard to focus on keeping the shop afloat." She picked up her mug of coffee and sipped. "Of course, it didn't seem to bother my ex as much as it did me, the louse. His stupid sporting store is doing as well as ever."

Alarm bells rang inside me, and I sucked in a giant breath. Melody was the wife! Did Verity even understand who she'd referred to me? Quickly, I tried to compose myself, as though I didn't have a thousand questions ricocheting in my head. "I'm sure your ex is upset, too. Sometimes people just show it differently." Like killing gossipy ladies who ratted out their indiscretions that led to a breakup.

Melody waved me off. "You know how men are."

Apparently, I didn't. Still, I offered a soft chuckle of agreement. "So, your husband owns the sporting goods store. What's his name again?"

"I hadn't said." She gazed dolefully into her mug. "His name is Rick. Anyway, I need to make my business a success—it's all I'll have left when everything is said and done."

"A divorce can be a terrible hardship."

Melody's fingers tightened around the mug. "You don't know the half of it. The hardest part was having the entire town talking about us. All the rumors and innuendos." She let out a gust of air.

"But that's all over now, thankfully." Her jaw tightened with unspoken words.

Maybe it hadn't been Rick that snuck down the back hallway and into the ice cream shop to kill Ruby—maybe it was Melody. Ruby had told me Rick's wife didn't want to hear about his choice of "extracurricular activities." Had Ruby's talking driven Melody over the edge?

Yet…if the couple was already split up, as Melody suggested, then the rumors and gossip would have taken place a while ago. Why wait so long to take action?

Unless Melody had simply seized an opportune moment.

My mind scrambled for a way to ask where she'd been two days ago when the murder took place. I relaxed my shoulders and tried to appear calm. "So, where were you two days ago?"

That didn't come out right.

"I mean," I said, trying to recover my fumble, "during all the excitement downtown." I leaned in. "There was a gunshot and so much commotion. Your shop is on the north side of the square, isn't it? That's pretty close by." There…smooth like butter.

Melody peered at me, eyes narrow. "Yes, it's between the used bookstore and that self-defense studio. They make a lot of noise." She made a moue of distaste.

Instead of responding, I waited for her to speak again to fill the uncomfortable silence—a trick I'd picked up from the crime dramas I'd recently started watching.

Melody's fingers worked the handle of the coffee mug. "As it happens, I was at my ex's store when all that went down. Unfortunately, I still need to see him from time to time because even though our marriage is ending, we're still officially business partners."

"I can't imagine how difficult that must be." She was a better woman than I not to walk away and let his ship sink. Much like I hoped the shoe company I used to work for was tanking without me there, as petty as it sounded. The only way I would know for sure is if I started talking to James again, which I had mostly decided not to do.

Melody adjusted the scarf around her neck, which seemed entirely too warm for the fall weather. "We're trying to untangle all our business dealings, but until then, I guess I have to put up with him. I try to keep my visits to his stupid store down to once a week. Unfortunately, I just happened to pick the wrong day."

Or the right one, if she'd wanted to get rid of someone who'd caused them grief.

I smiled. "Hopefully, I can help you build your brand so that you'll be super successful without the louse."

She toasted me with her mug. "On that note, I need to get back to the store. When can I expect to hear from you?"

"Based on the info you gave me, I can draw up some ideas and get back to you early next week." I turned off my tablet. "Right now, I have to focus on the grand reopening of Crumb's. It's this weekend." I noted the cute signage around the bakery announcing the upcoming festivities. "You'll be sure to stop by, won't you?"

Melody stood and adjusted the knit cuffs on her wrists. "I wouldn't miss it."

<hr>

MY NEXT APPOINTMENT was less eventful but likely to yield more monetary rewards in the long run. Naomi sent me the owner of an outdoor adventure camp that had already garnered national attention for its daring escapades. How she knew Jacob Rhine, I had no idea, considering the riskiest thing she ever did was play six cards at a time on bingo night.

"Can you give me a ballpark figure for your upgraded package?" Jacob's half-mast eyelids gave him the appearance of someone too chill to get ruffled by much. That was probably why he could do all the cool things depicted on his website, like parasailing, mountaineering, and skydiving, without having a heart attack.

"Since you already have quite a bit of social media in place, I can probably sign you on with my hourly rate." I crunched a few numbers while he sat back and drank his coffee unsweetened, like a Neanderthal.

"Are we about done here?" His thumb skated over the face-plate of his phone. "Looks like the tour group I have today is coming in early."

"Sure. I can email you with the details."

His thumb zipped across his phone even faster. "Dude, that is *sick*."

"What?" I craned my neck to see his cell.

Jacob shook his head. "Just looking at the city's page, and people are talking about that dead lady."

My interest piqued. "You mean Ruby?"

He looked at me. "You know her?"

"Didn't everyone? I mean, it *is* Beaver Bluff."

"I guess." He dimmed his phone and stuffed it into the pocket of his flannel shirt. "She was a mean old bat, but no one actually needs to say it online. Know what I mean?"

"I've heard she was pretty bad." I switched off my tablet.

Jacob snorted. "True, but we really shouldn't speak ill of the dead." He rapped the table and stood. "Hit me up later with the numbers." And with that, he left, nearly bumping into a wind-blown Verity.

"What was that all about?" she asked, unloading her purse and lightweight jacket onto the chair Jacob vacated.

"My new client."

"That's not the one I sent you."

"I know." I gaped at her. "Did you realize who the lady is that came by earlier?" I glanced around at the people scattered across other tables and lowered my voice. "She's the sporting goods guy's wife."

"Of course I know. That's why I sent her to you." Verity wrinkled her nose at me. "Didn't you see my text?"

I patted the non-existent pockets on my skirt. "Wait, where's my phone?" I reached inside my handbag and pawed around until I found it. "Oops, I forgot to turn it back on last night after James texted me."

Verity's eyes narrowed. "Do *not* tell me you texted him back."

"Okay, I won't."

She folded her arms. "You mean you didn't text him, or you won't tell me you texted him?"

"I didn't text him." *And* I wouldn't tell her if I had. I powered up the phone, which started pinging with incoming notifications, few of which actually mattered. "Anyway, you're not going to believe this." I gathered up all my belongings. "Let's go into the break room. We have a lot to talk about."

We hustled past a few customers and a bored-looking Krystal and through the kitchen. In the break room, the gang huddled around the table, having a meeting without us. Naomi and Polly bickered over a pad of paper filled with scribbles and scrawls that looked suspiciously like a suspect list. Aunt Lulu sat to the side, trying to get a word in edge-wise.

"What's going on here?" I scowled at the trio, then stepped closer to scan the sheets of paper. "I thought we all agreed not to get anywhere near the whole murder thing."

Lulu had the grace to turn red, while Polly and Naomi pointed at each other and said, "She did it!"

"I'm ashamed of you." I tutted. "To think that after the lecture you gave me, that you'd go ahead and butt into the investigation." Never mind that Verity and I were doing the same thing.

The three of them burst into a chorus of blame with the words "murder," "clue," and "hussy" all coming out at once— though the hussy one I couldn't place to save my life.

Verity whistled, which seemed wholly unnecessary, given the close proximity. "Ladies, ladies. Please." She perched her folded hands atop her chest. "It seems that we've *all* been poking around in this matter."

A collective gasp went up from the three ladies at the table.

The cacophony ensued once again, but this time, the hostile crowd turned on me.

Lulu's voice broke through. "But you promised."

"No, no, no." I tried to recall my exact words. "I don't believe promises were made, as such."

Verity cleared her throat. "Be that as it may, I think we all want the same thing, don't we?" She looked around the room, making eye contact with each one of us.

Reluctantly, the ladies grumbled in agreement, much to my relief.

"KC and I realize there's a certain risk that comes with trying to figure out the truth behind what's happening—"

"I just don't think it has to be up to us." Lulu folded her arms across her bosom.

"That's not what it sounded like a minute ago when you were floating theories. You had every bit as much to say as we did." Polly motioned between herself and Naomi.

"I had a few ideas—that's all." Lulu blinked innocently.

"We have to clear Walter's name." Naomi stabbed her finger against the table to punctuate each word.

Verity made a calming motion with her hands. "Look, we can't turn on each other now, so let's talk about this. Everyone has a vested interest in finding out who really killed Ruby."

Some of us had more of a vested interest than others, apparently.

"What exactly are you trying to say?" Lulu's eyebrows flexed in question.

It was clear where this was going, and really, it seemed inevitable. I looked around the small break room at the people who'd become my family. The only people I really trusted in the whole world. "It means that we have to quit hiding our efforts from each other and actually work together."

Chapter Ten

THE FACT I had real work to do was a little disappointing. Not that I didn't adore Aunt Lulu and want to have counter duties at Crumb's in addition to preparing for the grand reopening. That said, my time would be better spent promoting the grand reopening, sorting decorations, and finalizing the menu selections.

Instead, I worked the line alongside Krystal, my mind bobbing between the people and places associated with Ruby. Once everyone in the gang came clean with the fact that we were all butting into the investigation, each of us had a piece to talk about. Unfortunately, we needed to put off the discussion until this evening when we had more time—and privacy.

Finally, the line dwindled.

Krystal adjusted her long black ponytail, moroseness pouring off her in waves that I'd learned not to take personally. "I'm taking a break now if you don't mind."

Only a handful of customers sat inside the bakery, and none of them looked ready to storm the counter. "Not at all. I think I can hold down the fort." I turned to the only customer in the queue—Holly, the rental agent for my house. "Hey, there. What can I get for you?"

"I need the largest coffee ever." The petite blonde plopped her handbag on the counter. "And load it with cream and sugar." She offered a tired smile. "Just don't tell Griff."

I snickered. "Your secret is safe with me. I don't know how he can keep such a strict food and exercise regimen all the time."

"We're both technically on it since the wedding's coming up. But a little extra something never hurt anyone, if you know what I mean." She winked conspiratorially. "I'm burning the candle at both ends with all the planning."

The aroma of dark roasted coffee filled the air as I poured her a large with enough room for a generous helping of half-and-half. "Here you are."

She paid with a touchless credit card, then took a lengthy sip. "This hits the spot."

"You and Griff are coming to the grand reopening this weekend, right?" I wiped down the counter.

Holly nodded. "He told me about it after you saw him at the grocery store."

"Yeah, Verity and I were picking up a little something to take to Ruby's grandson. We feel terrible for him." Considering his rumpled appearance when we saw him at his house, I really did feel bad. That did not, however, clear him off my suspect list.

"Right? Those two were joined at the hip." Holly took a longer swig. "I'm just not sure what we're going to do about the rental agreement."

I stopped wiping the counter. "What rental agreement? I assumed Ruby owned her house."

"Not the house." Holly held up a finger as she took another drink. Then she leaned closer and bit her lip. "I probably shouldn't have said anything since it's not public knowledge."

"Well, so far, you haven't." I offered a quiet chuckle. "But whatever it is, it's just between us."

"It's probably not a big deal, but I think it would embarrass Walter if word got out. He's such a sweet man. I'd hate for that to happen."

"Did you say, Walter?" I whispered. "I'm confused."

"About a year ago, his shop was about to go under, so Ruby helped him out. I think she wanted a romantic relationship with him. Anyway, she bought out most of the business until he could get back on his feet. The lease for the shop is in her name—or at least the name of her trust, or whatever legal stuff she has set up. I'm not sure what happens now, to tell you the truth." She shrugged. "Who knows? Maybe it'll all go back to Walter."

My head exploded.

Quick, act casual.

"Well," I said as I resumed wiping the already-clean counter. "I guess we'll have to wait and see."

"Definitely. But I shouldn't have said anything because of client confidentiality, so don't tell anyone." She pinned me with her blue gaze.

"You can count on me to keep it quiet." Unless, of course, I needed to reveal it because of the investigation. For the greater good and whatnot.

THE GANG and I convened at my place as soon as Verity finished her shift at the library and Lulu turned over the closing duties to Krystal and Bert, who I'd only seen a few times. Leftover scones, coffee cake, and tarts on a revolving platter made up our evening snacks in lieu of my taking the time to cook dinner. It was more important to spend time on the case—and playing with Pooh Bear.

"Ladies, if I could have your attention?" Verity stood in front of an easel.

Everyone stopped mid-bite to gaze up at the dry erase board with a headline that said *Ruby's murder* in swirly pink letters. While the penmanship seemed a bit jovial for the occasion, it was better than the bubble font she'd used for the last crime board.

"As you can see, I didn't have time to fill in what we currently know about Ruby's death." Verity motioned with the dry erase marker. "But I think we can put our heads together and come up with some good ideas."

"That's not how they do it in all those cozies I read." Naomi shook her head.

Polly's eyebrows peaked. "You're reading cozies now?"

"Yeah, the British ones." Naomi's voice took on a mysterious quality. "All the amateur sleuths set up a crime board, but they do it so they can pin up new clues and suss out the killer."

"Suss out the killer?" Aunt Lulu used her fingers for air quotes.

Naomi nodded solemnly. "They do a *lot* of sussing."

"We can suss, too, using *this* board." The marker squeaked as Verity drew a checkmark next to Ruby's name. "We can swap it out later if we need to."

Polly flashed a skeptical look. "Naomi might be right. We need to pin things up."

I stood and went to Verity's side. "We don't actually need to pin things right *now*."

"But I brought these pictures—"

"Me too—"

"All I could find was a picture of a rope."

The ladies started digging through their purses and producing photos. I didn't even want to know how Polly got a shot of David sunning himself by his backyard pool.

"Okay, okay, okay." I clapped my hands. Everyone stopped talking, and Pooh Bear whined. "We can use tape. The important thing is to figure out who our prime suspects are and start…sussing."

For the next few minutes, I taped up David, Ella, and Melody —the last one based on the info I'd revealed to them after my quick meeting with her earlier at Crumb's. Her husband also belonged on the board too, as far as I was concerned, but no one had his picture. Unfortunately, I also wanted to include Walter—

needed to, really—but I wasn't quite prepared to battle the gang, even with my new intel. Perhaps I'd share with Verity what Holly told me, and we could investigate privately, at least until we were working with something solid.

"David seems like the most likely suspect to me," Polly said matter-of-factly.

Verity frowned. "After visiting with him, I'm not really sure about that. You should have seen how torn up he was about his grandma. His grief was so raw." The longing in Verity's voice was palpable.

"Oh, brother." Polly rolled her eyes. "Just because you insist on telling the whole truth all the time doesn't mean other people aren't deceitful, especially when it suits their purposes."

"You should have seen how grateful he was when KC handed him the tub of potato salad." Verity doodled a potato next to his head on the board, though I couldn't see what it had to do with the case.

"Wait—you took a tub of potato salad when you went to offer your condolences?" Lulu looked around my small living room, incredulous. "I thought I raised you better than that." Her gaze bounced between all the others. "Didn't I raise her better than that?"

"You certainly did." Naomi patted Lulu's knee.

"I'm not one to complain, but she could have at least made us sandwiches or something tonight." Polly shrugged. "I mean, slap a little peanut butter on the bread—"

"Excuse me." My defenses rose. "Let's take a moment to focus on my good qualities, like the fact that I'm doing my best to figure out what happened to Ruby so that Walter doesn't go to prison." *Unless he's guilty.* "Now, David is on the board because we all think he has the most to gain financially from Ruby's death."

"Where was he when she was murdered?" Lulu asked.

"He says he was having his hair cut." I took the marker and drew scissors next to the potato, which I would erase later.

"I'm sure that's exactly what he was doing." Verity snatched the marker back.

"Let's find out. There's only one barbershop and two salons in town. All we have to do is ask around." Naomi fluffed her white hair. "I can ask at my salon tomorrow."

Verity's eyebrows crouched low as she wrote *verify haircut* next to the scissors on the board. "Let's focus on Ella now. Yesterday, she told me and KC that she was at the grocery store at the time of the murder. How can we check on that?"

"I still don't think it's her," Polly insisted.

"Ruby drove her out of business." Lulu leaned forward and studied the board. "She seems like as good a suspect as any. Maybe I can ask around at the store when I pick up my special order tomorrow."

Verity wrote *verify shopping* next to Ella's name. "Man, this would sure be a lot easier if we had the same resources the police do."

"Like what?" Polly asked.

Naomi's eyes widened. "Like access to all the security cameras around town."

"Security cameras?" Lulu scrunched her nose. "How many do you think there are in Beaver Bluff?"

"Well, in my British novels, cameras are all over the place."

"Be that as it may, we have to work with what we have." I took the marker from Verity, wishing we had more than one. "Melody said she was at the sporting goods store when Ruby was murdered. Because Ruby talked about Melody last Friday night at bingo, I'm thinking the fallout from all the gossip Ruby started was bigger than I thought. Knowing that there's a back hallway that connects all the stores, she could have easily gone the back way and murdered Ruby while everyone was across the street when the gun went off."

"For that matter, Ella could have too." Verity grabbed the marker and wrote *verify sports shop* next to Melody's name.

"How does everything connect? I thought their stores led to an alley, like we have behind Crumb's." Lulu looked puzzled. "Maybe you can draw a diagram since you were back there, then we could better understand."

Verity handed over the marker. I drew the layout in as much detail as I could, with the three stores lined up—sporting goods, ice cream shop, and bistro—and the hallway that ran behind them. "As you can see, there was opportunity for someone to sneak out the back door, down the hallway, into Yum Yum's, murder Ruby, and sneak back out without anyone seeing."

Polly groaned. "Big problem…how would whoever was in either store even know Ruby was there, much less that they wouldn't be seen sneaking in and out?"

Oh, I hadn't thought of that.

I bit my lip, trying to conjure up an answer. "Well, for now, we'll have to work on the possibilities and go from there."

"I still don't like this." Aunt Lulu's expression tightened as she crossed her arms. "I think we need to leave it to the police. Now it's not just KC who could get hurt, but any one of you."

"But think of Walter." The concern in Naomi's voice made me wince. "The only cop I trust is Hamson, and KC already told us he's not really handling the case."

"The state police came in since Beaver Bluff doesn't have a detective anymore," I confirmed. "They seem like by the book people, so maybe we could give them a chance." Then, at least that way, I wouldn't have to break it to the gang that Walter was at the top of my suspect list.

Naomi adamantly shook her head. "I will not leave this to anyone else. Once we figure some things out, we can take it to the police and at least get them on the right trail. It can't hurt to do a little digging."

"For once, I'm with her." Polly hitched her thumb at Naomi. "And if all the rest of you want to bow out, we'll go it alone."

That couldn't end well.

As if reading my thoughts, Pooh Bear whined and laid his head on Polly's lap. I drew a long, slow breath. "We'll do the best we can without getting in too deep." I turned to my aunt and clasped my hands in front of my chest. "I think we can handle this."

Her mouth puckered, and worry lined her face. "Fine, but you have to keep it hush-hush."

Chapter Eleven

BEFORE I SENT them home last night, the gang and I divvied up duties that mostly involved checking alibis for our prime suspects. Lulu and Verity both had to work in the morning, leaving the sleuthing to the rest of us. And since Naomi and Polly said they couldn't miss water aerobics, citing the fact they had to maintain their girlish figures, that left me to get things started. So I decided to dig a little deeper into Melody's story by visiting her yarn store as soon as it opened.

Music with pan pipes and light drumming played overhead inside the shop, which was almost enough to send Melody to the top of my suspect list for the annoyance factor alone. Fortunately for her, I was more analytical than that. I was here for hard evidence, under the guise of taking pictures for the fall fiber event.

"May I help you?" A tiny brunette clad in flannel—the official uniform of Beaver Bluff, it seemed—came out from behind the counter.

I held up my phone. "I'm here to take a few pictures for your upcoming event, and if Melody has a minute, I'd like to chat with her."

"Ohhh." The woman's mouth formed a perfect circle. "I'm afraid you've missed her. She ran down to the sports store." She swept her arm around the shop. "But feel free to take as many photos as you'd like. We're a bit slow this morning, so your timing is good."

Not for sleuthing.

"Thanks, I'll do that." Disappointed, I turned away from the clerk and gazed around for the best light. Might as well work on my *actual* business, given the fact the nest egg I'd built up over the years wouldn't last forever if I didn't start generating an income.

Skeins of yarn in every color were nestled in bins along the walls. Wool, cotton, bamboo, acrylic—an array of choices for those lucky ladies crafty enough to knit up socks and shawls and blankets. I found baskets of yarn in fall colors near the window and started framing shots. Then I moved on to other features around the store, including the cozy nook at the back where groups were welcome to meet.

Maybe Melody wasn't Ruby's killer after all. How could a cold-blooded murderer create such a warm and inviting shop?

After a few minutes of photographing yarn—which made a surprisingly good subject—I waved goodbye and rushed outside. No way did I want to miss Melody down at the sporting goods store. The wind kicked up as I scurried across the town square. A few people waved when I went by, and I nodded in return while clutching the folds of my skirt.

When I crossed the street, I noticed that Walter's shop, right next door to the sporting goods place, had finally reopened. Maybe I'd stop in there next, seeing as how I had to investigate him on the sly.

I blew into A Good Sport with a gust of wind that sent brochures on the cash wrap flying to the floor. "Oops, sorry about that." I hurried to scoop them up.

"It's cool." The same teen I'd seen the last time I was here handled the cash register. He swept the mop of hair out of his eyes. "Can I help you find something?" His tone indicated he'd rather I said no.

"Actually, I'm here to see Melody. Is she around?" I smoothed my errant strands of hair as I checked out his nametag.

"She's with the boss man in the back." Ryan tapped his side pocket, where I imagined his phone was begging to be played with when no one was looking. Though he didn't strike me as someone who paid close attention to his surroundings, I didn't want to stereotype. He could very well have a nugget of information if he was here the day of the murder.

"So," I said, trying to think of a lead-in. "There's been a lot of action around here lately, eh?"

Ryan offered a one-shoulder shrug. "I guess."

"I mean, were you here when that gun went off? I was right outside eating ice cream." I feigned wiping sweat off my forehead. "That was scary. Then my dog ran across the street to see what was happening, so I had to follow."

Ryan's face lit with a genuine smile. "Is your dog that big one that hangs out next door?"

"Yeah, his name is Pooh Bear."

"That dude is *lit*."

"Right?" Finally, I had a connection. "So, he drags me across the street, and I see that man that shot his own foot."

"I was there too." Ryan laughed, then immediately sobered. "I guess that's not really funny, but c'mon."

"Wait, if you were across the street, who was watching the store?" I tilted my head.

"Boss lady was here and said I could go check it out, and she'd hold down the fort. She's pretty chill."

Assuming *boss lady* meant Melody, then her story checked out. "Sounds like she's cool and stuff."

Ryan paused. "Weird thing was, she wasn't here when I came back. Whatever, though, it's her store. Well, her and the boss man." He tapped his pant pocket again. "Are you going to wait for them?"

"Yeah, maybe I'll just have a look around until they come out." I meandered away from the cash wrap toward the climbing gear at the back of the store. When I got to the aisle with all the clippy things and ropes, voices rose from the office area near the hallway.

Quickly, I scurried toward the hubbub on the toes of my shoes so as not to let my heels clack on the floor. I pressed my back against the wall, just out of Ryan's line of sight and close enough to the door to hear Melody's terse voice.

"Do you really think you're so special that you can do whatever you want without answering to anyone?"

Rick, or at least a man I presumed to be Melody's husband, scoffed. "Give it a rest. The jig's up."

"What jig? Quit talking stupid."

"After what happened, and you're calling *me* stupid?" This time, he grunted.

"All I can say is that you're not going to get away with it. If I go down, so are you." Her footsteps sounded, and the office door whisked open. She stormed out and stood in front of me, eyes wild.

"Hi," I squeaked past the knot in my throat. My heart tripped into overtime as I waited for her to speak.

"What are you doing here?"

"It's me, KC." Perhaps the dumbest thing I'd said all week. Of course she knew who I was, but at the moment, with her shoulders heaving and her expression tight, it didn't look like she cared.

Melody's mouth flexed in different directions, and she raked her knit cuff-clad hand through her hair. She flicked a glance behind her, then reached back to shut the door. "Right, sorry. I didn't expect to see you."

Despite my heart thumping against my ribcage, I mustered a smile and slid into professional mode. I'd process what I'd overheard later. Slowly, I reached into my handbag and pulled out my phone. "I wanted to show you these pictures I took of your store just now." I unlocked my cell and opened the gallery. "These are going to look great on your social channels leading up to your event."

"Great, yes." Melody pinched the bridge of her nose. "I can't do this right now. Please, call first next time." With that, she stormed out the back door.

So much for my fuzzy feelings at the yarn shop. Melody just moved herself to the top of my list.

"Did you find her?"

I startled. I'd been so caught up in Melody, I hadn't heard Ryan sneak up behind me. "Yeah. She seemed a little...out of sorts. I'll just be going." I edged past the young clerk and walked up the main aisle on shaky legs.

Outside, I stood on the sidewalk and waited a moment for my eyes to adjust to the light. What was that all about? Melody basically threatened her husband that if she went down, so would he. Were they in on Ruby's murder together? Had she done it, and he aided and abetted by encouraging her or covering it up?

On the other hand, maybe it was typical divorce-type fighting. There was no way to know for sure. Or was there? Maybe I could get somewhere by talking to the ex-husband. I generally had good luck getting men to spill the beans. After being chewed out by Melody, Rick might enjoy the opportunity to vent.

A familiar figure on the right caught my attention. Two stores down, I watched David open the door and go inside Uptown Locks Salon. Of the three places in town for haircuts, this was the last one I'd think he'd go to. Although it was the most expensive, so it made a little bit of sense. But why would he go for another cut so soon after the last one?

Melody all but forgotten, I hustled down the sidewalk, careful to keep a low profile. Then I waited a few beats before peering through the window, where I saw a young woman leading him away from the reception area. There was only one way to see why he was there.

It looked like I'd have to take one for the team and get my hair done—for the good of the investigation.

UPTOWN BOASTED TEN STATIONS, each with a five-foot-high privacy screen, a separate area for mani/pedis—note to self for a future appointment—and a coffee bar. The smooth jazz playing through the overhead speakers and a burbling fountain were almost enough to drown out the hum of hair dryers.

I leaned close to the receptionist but kept my eye on David, who disappeared behind the third station on the right. Clearly, he was getting his hair cut, even after telling us he'd already had it done. "Is it possible to get an appointment? Maybe just a quick trim."

"Hmm…normally we're booked solid. Let me see." She flipped through an old-timey book that appeared to be smudged with hair dye. "Do you have a stylist you normally see?"

Yes, back in LA.

I pointed to the vacant station next to David's. "How about that one?"

The receptionist gave me a puzzled look. "O-kay…let me check." She wandered over to the stylist who sat in the seat, flipping through a magazine, then came back. "Sheila will take you."

Quickly, I scurried over to the station, hoping I didn't miss anything David said. Not that he'd admit to murdering his grandmother while having his hair done. Although I'd heard that a good stylist can get a client to admit just about anything.

I sat in the chair, straining to hear David's muffled voice on the other side of the privacy screen.

"What can I do for you today? So glad you came in. I just had a cancellation, and that literally never happens. Honestly, I'm hustling from the time I get here until the time I leave." Sheila, never pausing for a breath, swiveled me around to face the mirror. She tugged at my strands, her nose wrinkling. "Let me guess… highlights? I can whip your hair into shape in no time."

I offered a flimsy smile. "Sure."

"Feels like so long since I've been here." David's voice drifted over the screen. "Anyway, you can't begin to imagine. I had no idea when Gran died it—"

"Would you like to go with the same color you have on the ends here?" Sheila cut in as she fluffed a black cape over me and clipped it in the back.

"Whatever you think," I spoke quickly and hoped Sheila would stay quiet.

"So, tell me about yourself. Are you new to Beaver Bluff?" Sheila tucked a neck strip inside the cape.

"I just…" I motioned to my head. "I'm a little headachy." An imaginary Verity internally scolded me for the lie. She had no idea how hard it was to tell the absolute truth while trying to investigate. It simply couldn't be done.

"Ah, gotcha. Let's just get this sorted." She grabbed color swatches of hair and held them up to my head, looking at each one with a thoughtful gaze.

"Before she died, my grandma was telling me she had this eerie feeling of—"

"What about this one?" Sheila displayed the swatch near my face. "I think this would bring out those beautiful tones in your eyes."

"Sure, sure." I agreed without actually looking.

"But I told her, Gran, you can't really be—"

"This color palette will brighten up your features. Sometimes that helps as we get into the colder weather and fall sets in." Sheila grabbed supplies. "I mean, don't get me wrong, I love this time of year."

"My head, remember?" I pointed to my temple and winced.

"Oh, right." She nodded solemnly and lowered her voice to a whisper.

"So, I need to meet with Gran's lawyer later. There's a lot to—"

"Then after that, we'll have just enough time for a trim." Sheila kept to a whisper, but it was enough to drown out David's voice. Despite my pleas for quiet, my stylist rambled on, content to discuss the weather, her days in beauty school, and the outfit change for the high school mascot. My headache claim had come true—maybe that was my punishment for lying.

The only concrete words I caught from David were him agreeing to a "much deserved quick pedicure" as soon as his cut was finished. Unfortunately, that was about the same time my hair was properly foiled, and Sheila situated me under the dryer.

Bored, I decided to get a little work done. My to-do list had grown, given the fact I was adding potential clients without actually doing any work. I clicked through Trudi's social media first and added a pity heart to those of her three faithful followers—Erman, Mary, and Tom—noting the blandness of her animal photos. Then I made notes and moved on to Jacob's adventure camp social channels. The pics he took himself seemed better than anything I could do, but his hash-tagging and captions could use some work, as well as a cohesive strategy to pull in new clients.

The hot air on my head made me perspire. Sheila stood across the salon, holding someone else hostage with conversation. I was pretty sure she forgot about me.

"Is that you, KC?" Naomi squinted at me from the front door.

"What are you doing here?" I lifted the dryer off my head, stood, and glanced around before hustling over to Naomi and Polly near the reception area.

"Us?" Polly motioned to herself. "What are *you* doing here?"

"Yeah, *we* were on salon duty for checking alibis." Naomi turned to Polly. "Weren't we?"

I tried to usher them back outside, but they stayed planted in the reception area. In my peripheral vision, I saw David coming towards us. I motioned my hand to my neck. "Shhhhh."

Polly nodded. "I distinctly remember before we left last night that *we* were checking out salons."

"That's what I thought too." Naomi grimaced at me. "Don't you trust us?"

My stomach clenched as David approached.

He flashed us a wary gaze. "Checking out salons?"

I chuckled. "Yeah, I needed some…touch-ups. And I don't have a regular salon."

"Interesting." His eyes narrowed.

I folded my arms over my cape. "So…two haircuts in one week?" As long as he saw me, I had to use it to my advantage by putting him on the defensive.

"Excuse me?" David slapped his hand to his chest. "I think you need to mind your own business." His gaze volleyed between Polly, Naomi, and me. Then, disgruntled, he left the salon.

"Well," I said, gazing between my cohorts. "David has some explaining to do."

Chapter Twelve

"WHAT HAPPENED TO YOU?" Polly put on her readers, leaned close, and peered at me.

I touched my head self-consciously. "I don't know what you're talking about."

"Your hair." She looked at Lulu, Naomi, and Verity, all seated around the break room table. "She looks like a zebra."

"Polly!" Everyone gasped in unison.

"What?" Her eyes darted around the room, then she shrugged. "I said what I said."

Polly wasn't wrong. Apparently, I should have paid closer attention to Sheila when she rambled on about my color choices. Instead of subtle caramel highlights, she gave me platinum stripes that ran in stark lines down the length of my hair. I'd managed to escape the salon before Polly and Naomi were finished with their manicures, but apparently, I couldn't hide from them forever.

"I don't know. It's kind of…trendsetting." Naomi reached out and patted my hand.

Lulu nodded. "That's right. KC has always been ahead of the curve."

Polly raised her eyebrows and smirked. "What do *you* think, Verity?"

Everyone huddled close and eyed Verity.

She swallowed, and her mouth formed silent words before she finally spoke aloud. "I think…I think…" She licked her lips. "I think we should talk about what KC learned at the salon…before the incident."

Polly slapped her hands together. "I knew it. All I did was say what everyone was thinking, but you all ganged up on me."

"Ganged up on *you?*" I tucked errant strands behind my ears. "I'm the one whose hair has just been upgraded to an *incident.*" I drew a deep breath to compose myself. Incident or not, we had a lot of ground to cover before Verity had to get back to the library, and I needed to work the counter with Krystal. "Never mind my hair. We have bigger issues to deal with." Some of which I had no intention of revealing to the group before I had more proof. The ladies would pulverize me if I mentioned Walter's suspicious financial connection to Ruby.

"Indeed, we do. David lied, plain and simple." Polly's hand sliced the air with finality. "He just moved to the top of my list."

"She's right." Naomi nodded matter-of-factly.

Verity looked between the three of us who'd been at the salon. "What did he do?"

I glanced into the kitchen to make sure we were alone, then I lowered my voice. "He didn't have his hair cut the day Ruby was murdered like he'd told us. He had it cut today."

Verity covered her mouth. "There must be some misunderstanding."

"Nope, I was there for the whole thing. I was coming out of the sporting goods store—I'll tell you about that in a second—and I saw him go into that Uptown salon, so I followed him." I fingered my hair. "I was trying to listen in on his conversation from one station over, so I only heard parts of what he said, but Naomi is right. David lied."

"Boy, he was furious when you called him out on it, too," Naomi said.

Verity scowled at me, then quickly changed the subject. "In

that case, good luck getting any more information out of him. Now tell us what happened at the sporting goods place."

"After taking some pictures at the yarn store, I went down to see Melody." I recalled the scene in my head, trying to remember all the incriminating words I'd heard her and Rick sling when they thought no one was listening. "In the back office, Melody and her soon-to-be-ex-husband were having an argument."

"I knew there was something fishy about her." Lulu took a swig of her tea and shook her head. "But I don't know if it equates to murder."

"She said, 'if I go down, you're going with me.' Or something like that." If only I'd turned on my phone's recorder. There was a lot more to sleuthing than I realized, but I'd know for the next time I was listening to a conversation when I wasn't supposed to. I stirred more sugar into my coffee, remembering the venom in her voice. "What else could she have meant? Melody and her husband should be at the top of the list." Except for Walter, only I didn't know how to find out if he was as innocent as everyone thought.

Naomi stared around the table intently. "KC's right. Melody and Rick should be at the top of the list."

Lulu turned to Naomi. "KC and Polly can't both be right."

"You're right, too." Naomi offered a one-shoulder shrug.

"We just don't have enough information." Verity closed her eyes and rubbed her temples. "We can't prove that Melody and her husband were so upset with Ruby that they wanted to kill her, and we definitely can't prove that David had a motive. Ruby gave him a pretty good life."

"True. But we *do* know that David wasn't where he said he was when it happened, and we know that Melody had a motive and the opportunity." I swilled the creamy coffee in my mouth before continuing. "And get this, according to the kid who works there, Melody had agreed to watch the store while he ran across the street when the gun went off."

"So?" This, from Polly.

I looked each lady in the eye. "And when the guy got back, she wasn't there."

"Oh, boy." Lulu shifted in her seat. "Melody and David were both somewhere other than where they claimed, but that still doesn't mean either one is guilty."

"But they both look suspicious." Naomi squeezed Verity's hand. Apparently, she had sensed Verity's growing attachment to Ruby's grandson, too. "Sorry, but David really could be guilty."

So could Walter, I wanted to say but didn't.

I sat up and turned to Aunt Lulu. "Wait, did you find out anything at the grocery store about Ella?"

Lulu studied her teacup. "Well…not exactly. I tried asking around, but I felt so conspicuous."

"You had one assignment." Polly rolled her eyes.

"Let's not go there," Verity chimed in, giving the distinct impression she was irritated by Polly's accusations against David. "You and Naomi were supposed to be helping, and all you did was get gussied up."

"Gussied up, seriously? It's a standing appointment." Naomi flashed her nails. "You don't just skip."

"Ladies, please." I calmed them with my hands, wishing I'd gotten a manicure instead of highlights. "We've all made mistakes." I turned to the salon buddies and gave them a warning look. "Like talking about the case right there in the open. It's a wonder no one heard us. Anyway, the important thing is that we keep trying. But at this point, Verity's right. We don't have enough information yet on any front. All we can do is keep piecing together what we know and get this figured out."

The door between the kitchen and the front of the bakery swung open. Krystal called out. "KC, can you come help me? I've got a line."

"Be right there." I stood and grabbed a Have a Crummy Day apron from a hook on the wall. "Let's regroup tomorrow." I turned to Verity. "Can you meet me after work? We can pick up some ice cream."

Her eyes brightened. "Sure, as long as we can do some training afterward."

I smiled to hide my sigh. Ice cream was just a cover. It was time I let her in on my secret—before Walter potentially got away with murder.

KRYSTAL and I fell into an easy rhythm at the counter. Scones, tarts, coffee, tea—everything delicious that took all my self-control not to nibble between customers. The heavenly scent of blueberry muffins baking in the kitchen laced the air.

My cell buzzed inside my apron, but I ignored it until the after-lunch crowd dwindled and Krystal went on break with her husband, Clyde.

I thumbed the passcode on my phone and pulled up my notifications. Three texts from James. Deleting the messages without reading them wouldn't be a big deal. It wasn't like he still had a hold on me.

On the other hand, what if there were final details to clean up in regard to my old job? That would totally make sense, in which case I needed to read the texts.

I glanced around guiltily before opening the messages.

C'mon, KC—it wasn't what you thought.

I gave you more than a month to cool off.

When are you coming back? I miss you.

Rogue emotions roiled inside me as I stabbed my phone. Delete, delete, delete. Idiot expected me to believe he was innocent and trip all over myself to get back to LA. Why would I leave Beaver Bluff when I had my Crumb's family? They were more than enough, and once I landed my next career, I wouldn't lose touch like the last time I left town.

Speaking of which, I needed to get to the sign store and pick up the banners for the grand reopening, then I could head over to the ice cream shop to meet Verity. I had a million things to do, and none of them involved pining over a weasel with smooth words and a slick grin.

When Krystal finished her break, I took off. First, I stopped at home and picked up Pooh Bear. Then I headed back downtown and double-parked with my hazard lights on near the front door of the sign shop. I'd only be a minute, and Pooh Bear didn't like me out of his sight.

Inside, it took a moment for my eyes to adjust. Machines whirred in the back room, and the smell of ink hung faintly in the air. I hooked onto the end of the short line, hoping it would move quickly so I could get back to Pooh. While I waited, I updated the to-do list on my phone and rechecked the pictures in my photo gallery. I'd forgotten all about the shot of Ruby's appointment book.

Two meetings had been crossed off—one with Benson Michaels and another with Edith Jones. Who were they? I added a note to my to-do list to check them out.

The customer at the counter gathered up her signs and turned to leave. Her eyes brightened when she noticed me. "KC, I didn't see you standing there."

"Trudi—hey. Sorry I haven't gotten back to you yet." I wanted to add *call Trudi* to my to-do list but figured it best to wait until she left.

"No problem. You told me it would be a while." She held up her signs. "I was just picking these up for the adopt-a-pet day."

"Sounds like you're making progress." I thought back to the last time we met. "I feel bad that you were upset when you left Crumb's. I didn't mean to be the one to tell you about Ruby."

Trudi sighed mournfully. "It's not your fault I overreacted. It's just that she was a big supporter of the animal rescue. I'm just not sure how we're going to stay afloat now that she's gone."

I cuffed her shoulder and smiled. "I'm going to do everything I can to help you make the animal rescue a success. We'll make a great team."

"That's just it." Trudi bit her lip. "I'm not sure I can even pay you now."

Ouch. That didn't bode well for my business-building efforts. Yet, I still felt compelled to help the animals and trust it would be okay. "Don't worry. We'll work something out." I said goodbye to her just as the bell above the front door tinkled and Officer Leon walked in, her gait firm and confident.

"Ms. Crumb." The officer pulled off her sunglasses. "Is that your car double-parked outside?" Her raised eyebrow told me she already knew the answer.

I winced. "Let me just grab my signs—"

"I'd rather not have to ticket you." Her hand wheeled as if to make me hurry.

Thankfully, the clerk sped up and had my order on the counter. Without checking over the signs and verifying their accuracy, I paid and took the bundle, then followed Officer Leon outside.

Officer Hamson leaned against my car, scratching Pooh Bear's ears through the open window. Then he cooed in a voice that should've been for babies only. "I don't know why someone would leave you in the car all cooped up like that."

Pooh Bear wrinkled his forehead and released a sorry whine. Traitor.

"Nice to see you and my dog conspiring against me." I went to fold my arms, but my sign bag was too bulky.

Hamson straightened, pulled his hand to his side, and studied me. His mouth quirked. "What happened? You remind me of something."

If he said zebra, there would be another murder in Beaver Bluff.

"Never mind my hair."

Hamson regained his professional veneer. "Right. Anyway, is this your car?"

I rolled my eyes. "Obviously." I waited for the door to unlock automatically since the key fob was in my handbag, but when it didn't, I reached for the fob to unlock it manually. Then I tossed the signs into the backseat.

"You need to move this along immediately." He spoke in a deep tone, completely opposite the one he used for Pooh Bear. He waved his hands in a sweeping motion as if I needed direction on which way to pull out.

"I'm going, I'm going." I hustled around to the driver's side. "Thank you for keeping the streets of Beaver Bluff safe from double parkers." Then I muttered in a low voice. "At least we're safe from something."

"How's that?" Hamson came around and stood on the other side of my door, where we were practically nose to nose, thanks to my four-inch heels. "Did you have something to add, Ms. Crumb?"

"Oh, stop with the Ms. Crumb stuff." I scowled at him.

"What's that supposed to mean?" A hint of spicy cologne wafted off him in irritating waves.

"You're talking to me like you don't even know me." I slid my sunglasses on so he couldn't read my eyes. The last thing I wanted was to expose the fact I actually cared. Which I mostly didn't.

"I'm being professional."

"Well, that's one word for it."

Hamson matched my scowl. "We need to keep the streets clear. Your car is a hazard."

I thought back to last month after I'd solved the murder of Bronco Peters and the way Hamson's tough exterior had softened by a fraction. The concern in his eyes when he found out I'd been hurt, the way he came to my house to follow up with the good news after the real murderer was charged. We'd had a connection. I was sure of it. Unless it was simply the fact I'd been recently cast off, and I was an emotional wreck.

Maybe I'd read the situation all wrong. James Carlisle had me in knots then and was apparently still mixing me up now.

I slid behind the steering wheel and rolled down the window

before closing the door. "By the way, are you and those state police any closer to finding the killer?"

Hamson scrutinized me. "Why? What have you heard?"

"Aha."

"Don't aha me."

"You guys are no closer to finding out who killed Ruby than…." I stopped myself.

"Than who—you?" His eyes slivered, and he leaned into my car and spoke in a low tone. "Didn't I warn you to stay out of it? Those state police don't fool around. I can't keep them from hauling you in if you keep sticking your nose into this. And don't forget there's a killer who hasn't been caught yet. Remember what happened to you last time."

I smiled. Hamson did care if only a little. "I'm just checking to make sure you're keeping the streets of Beaver Bluff safe from double parkers *and* killers." Then I closed the door and waved goodbye, my heart a little lighter than it was before.

Chapter Thirteen

SOMETIMES ICE CREAM is the only solution to a problem, like figuring out if a trusted acquaintance is really a killer.

After dropping Pooh Bear off with Polly and Naomi, I got to the town square early. I hoped to catch Verity before we went inside the ice cream shop so I could give her a heads-up about Walter's financial entanglements with Ruby. The sun grazed the horizon while I sat on a park bench with my eye on Yum Yum's, and I wondered if Verity had forgotten our meeting. I sat back and listened to the wind whisper through the trees and the sound of kids playing on the grass behind me.

What if all our snooping was leading us nowhere? Sure, I had a solid list of suspects with flimsy alibis, but what did I really know? The killer could literally be anyone, and meanwhile, the gang and I were wasting our time, bumbling around in the dark.

Maybe my days would be better spent building my clientele and figuring out where I wanted to go in life.

"Sorry I'm late." Verity dropped her tote on the ground and sat. "I got held up by a patron with a really sticky research question. I didn't have any idea what it took to start an LLC and get things sorted out before starting a business. I learn something new every day."

I sat up and tried to look alert. "Glad you're here. I think Walter's about ready to close up shop for the day."

"Let's get inside, then. I need a sugar fix." She looked at me sternly and clarified. "A *small* fix."

"Wait." I held her arm to keep her from standing. Then I drew a deep breath, knowing what I had to say would not end well. "There's something you need to know before we go inside."

Verity's eyes narrowed with suspicion. "What?"

"I talked to Holly—you know, the property rental agent?"

"Obviously, I know Holly." Verity folded her arms, wise to my stall tactics. "Go on."

"Anyway, she mentioned she didn't know what was going to become of the Yum Yum's property agreement now that Ruby was dead."

Verity cocked her head, her demeanor changing quickly. "What does Ruby have to do with Walter's shop?"

"Apparently, he came on hard times a while back, and Ruby bailed him out. The lease was in her name and maybe part of the business, too. I think Holly was a little murky on that part."

Verity grinned. "That puts him in the clear, then. There's no way he'd want her dead if it put his shop in jeopardy."

"Not so." I shook my head. "It sounded like the way it was set up, Walter would gain back full control of his store once Ruby was out of the way."

"Are you sure about that?"

I wasn't sure about anything. "That's how Holly made it sound, but I'm guessing the details are buried in the legal stuff."

"There's no way that sweet old man is guilty of murder." She shook her head adamantly. "Remember how upset he was when it happened?"

The memory came back in stark detail—details I'd rather forget, like the way Ruby's face looked, mashed in her bowl of hot fudge. "Of course I remember. Think about it, though. He was sweating and shaky and nervous."

"Because someone was murdered in his shop."

"Or because *he'd* just murdered someone."

"If he wanted to kill Ruby, why would he do it at his own store?"

"Opportunity." I shrugged. "And so people would say exactly what you just did."

Verity rolled her eyes. "Fine. I still can't believe it, but let's just get this over with."

"At least we get ice cream out of the whole deal. Let's go." We crossed the street and entered the shop, where the smell of sugar laced the air.

"You two are a sight for sore eyes." Relief poured off Walter when he saw us. "I haven't had a customer all afternoon. This murder thing affected my store worse than I thought it would."

Wait—did he mean he actually thought about the consequences before he squeezed the life out of Ruby? I shook off the thought, not at all eager to keep him at the top of my suspect list but knowing he'd earned his spot. But maybe he meant he realized *after* her untimely demise that Yum Yum's would have a drop in business. I hoped that's what he meant.

A worried expression creased Walter's face as he wiped down a counter that was already clean. "Did you see the paper today?"

Come to think of it, I'd been so busy I hadn't checked the online version of the Beaver Bugle yet. Not a good move if I wanted to stay current on the case. "What'd it say? Were there any new leads?"

Walter rubbed his whiskered face. "No—at least not that the police are revealing to the public. But the paper dubbed the murderer the Ice Cream Killer." He closed his eyes as though it pained him. "Can you imagine that? The Ice Cream Killer. Just think what that's going to do to my business."

Clearly, he wasn't missing Ruby on a personal level, but I decided to let that slide. "That's part of why we're here." I slung my handbag over the back of a nearby chair—one I hoped hadn't been Ruby's death spot—and pulled out my tablet. "I think we should use social media to get people back in. I know you were reluctant to do that before, but maybe we could start small and build from there."

Walter's face sagged. "I've always relied on word of mouth."

"Social media is super similar," I assured him. "It's like word of mouth, but digital. It'll give you the social proof you need that things are back to normal here at the shop. Once people see others here, they'll come back too."

"I'll think about it. In the meantime, what can I get you, ladies? The usual?" His tepid smile tugged my heartstrings.

"Make mine a double."

Verity nudged me. "A double, *really*?" she said under her breath.

"I'm trying to help his business." I spoke through clenched teeth, then smiled sweetly at Walter when he looked up.

While he scooped our orders, I mentally scrambled for a way to nudge the truth out of him. There was no dispute that he had financial ties to Ruby, but how could I get him to tell us how deep those ties ran? Or what kind of legal ground he stood to gain from her death? The important thing was not to scare him off the way I'd scared David. This was going to take skill and finesse, a light touch to coax the facts from our friend.

"So," Verity said, plunking her elbow onto the glass case. "I hear you and Ruby were business partners."

Walter choked, dropping the cone and scoop into the carton of mint chocolate chip. He pulled back from the case and coughed into his elbow until his eyes watered. I wasn't at all sure I still wanted the ice cream after that. Even I had my limits.

"Are you okay?" I restrained myself from rounding the counter to slap his back.

He held up a finger and nodded. Finally, he stood and looked at Verity. "Sorry, but you caught me off guard."

She gasped. "It's true, then? You and Ruby were in business together?" She turned to me. "I didn't actually believe you."

It was my turn to gasp. "I only told you what I heard."

"Haven't we all learned anything from Ruby's death?" Walter

looked between the two of us. "Talking about others behind their backs is a terrible thing to do. Gossip is deadly." Walter rounded the counter, flipped the sign, and locked the door. Then ambled back to the table and sat across from Verity and me.

She spoke first. "What do you know about her death, and what does gossip have to do with it?"

With a somber face, he addressed us. "I don't know more than anyone else, but I do know this—she didn't endear herself to anyone with all the tales she told. There were a lot of people angry with Ruby for various reasons."

He wasn't telling us anything we didn't already know. I rubbed my eyes to fend off a headache. "So what, exactly, is your involvement?"

"There's no mistaking the fact that Ruby and I were not great friends, and I won't pretend otherwise."

Verity shot me a pointed look. "I appreciate a man who's willing to tell the truth. It's the only way to build trust."

"I do, as well." I volleyed the pointed look right back at her. Just because Walter implied complete honesty didn't mean he was free from secrets. Although, to be fair, I needed to hear him out before determining fact from fiction. The last thing I wanted was for a man we all liked to be guilty of murder.

He scooted his chair closer to the table. "A few months ago… no, I have to start further back." He scrubbed his cheeks with his hands and sighed. "Some years back, Ruby and I were nearly married."

I gasped, then quickly composed myself. "I had no idea."

Walter scratched his head, leaving his hair in white tufts on top. "No one did. It was what you kids call a whirlwind romance —I swept her off her feet."

It was hard to imagine anything or anyone sweeping Ruby off her feet. I tamped down the uncharitable thoughts. "Obviously, you didn't go through with it. Why?"

"First, you have to understand that Ruby wasn't always as gruff and grumpy as she is now…I mean, was." A smidgen of sorrow clouded his eyes. "Something about her changed after we broke it off."

"Was the break up mutual?" Verity scrutinized Walter.

His face pinched. "Not exactly. You see, I wasn't ready to make that kind of commitment, especially since David had just come to live with her. His parents more or less left him with his grandma, and he was troubled."

Concern camped in Verity's eyes. "In what way?"

"The usual stuff that teens can deal with—staying out late, attending a party or two."

I thought back to my high school days, both shuddering at the awkward memories and mining them for any that included Ruby's grandson. "Funny, but I don't remember David at Beaver Bluff High."

"You wouldn't because he didn't go there." Walter gazed toward the window. "He went to a private school a few miles up the coast. Maybe he'd have done better going to school here. At this point, who can say? The bottom line was that I wasn't ready to be a father figure."

If David was now in his thirties, that would have put Walter in his fifties at the time, at the youngest. Clearly, he'd decided he would *never* be ready to be a father, which I understood, given the fact I was staring forty in the face and still had no maternal instincts. Unless I counted Pooh Bear.

"Unfortunately, Ruby didn't take the breakup too well." Walter studied the table instead of looking at us.

"That's an understatement." I grabbed my tiny water bottle out of my handbag. "It looked to me like she still wanted more than a professional relationship."

"Is that why she helped you out with your shop?" There was nothing subtle about Verity's questioning.

Walter shrugged. "Maybe. Almost a year ago—in a moment of weakness, mind you—I let it slip to her that my shop was struggling." He pounded his fist on the table. "I knew better than to let her into the business, but I was desperate. It all seemed so simple."

"Romance and money rarely mix well." Verity shook her head and released a windy sigh.

"That's just it—there wasn't supposed to be any romance."

"But there was?" I wrinkled my nose, wondering if Naomi knew what she'd be getting into with this man.

"No. I insisted we go through a lawyer and keep everything on the up and up." He continued with his story. "I took the money as a loan and included her on the lease. Then David started to get involved, trying to advise her against it."

Which put Walter and David at odds, no doubt.

"But Ruby went ahead with our deal."

"So what happens now that she's dead?" Verity caught the harshness in her voice. "Sorry…passed away."

Walter hesitated, then looked around the small shop to stall. Finally, his gaze landed on us. "The loan is forgiven, and the shop is turned completely back over to me."

This time, it was Verity who gasped and covered her mouth.

"I know, I know." Walter held up his hands as though surrendering. "The whole thing looks bad."

Verity snorted. "You can say that again."

I laid my hand on her arm. "Let's give Walter the benefit of the doubt." At least until we were alone and could discuss the situation without the killer present. Not that I was making assumptions, much. On the other hand, would he be this forthcoming if he were guilty?

Walter nodded at me politely. "Thank you, KC. In any case," he continued, "I can assure you, I had nothing to do with Ruby's death, even if it looks suspicious. I've been waiting for the police to come back and interrogate me, but they haven't said a word so far. All I can think is that they haven't talked to Ruby's lawyer yet."

Which left a huge opportunity for Verity and me. And just like last time, the cops seemed to be missing critical clues. It really would be up to us to crack this case.

"Do you happen to know the lawyer's name?" I asked.

"Benson Michaels."

One of the names in Ruby's appointment book for the day after she was murdered. Interesting.

"Not only that, but she told me she planned on making some changes to her will." Walter tapped the table with his index finger. "Considering the trouble she and David were having lately, I can't help but wonder if she was ready to write him out."

Trouble? From the little I saw of their interaction, nothing indicated there was a problem. "I hadn't heard that. What kind of trouble were they having?"

Walter shook his head. "Remember what I said about gossip? It's not up to me to speak of someone else's issues."

Verity's expression was tight as she stood and secured her tote over her shoulder. "Thank you, Walter. We appreciate your candor."

Funny, because she didn't *seem* to appreciate his implicating David. But if what Walter said was true, perhaps David put an end to Ruby…before she could put an end to his lavish lifestyle.

Chapter Fourteen

"THAT WASN'T AT ALL what I expected." Verity slid on her sunglasses as Walter locked the door behind us.

"I had no idea Walter and Ruby were a couple. Even the idea of those two together blows my mind." I gazed at the sunset painting the evening sky with deep shades of pink and orange, lost in thought.

Verity linked arms with me as we strolled down the sidewalk. "Given what we know now, he really might be guilty."

"What?" I stopped walking and pulled away. "After all that? I'm less convinced now than before we talked to him."

She fisted her hand on her hip. "Now is not the time to lose your objectivity. Walter had the biggest motive and opportunity."

I tried to see her eyes behind the shades. "You just don't want to believe David could be guilty."

"Even if he was—which I doubt—you've scared David off. At this point, there's no way we can get more clues out of him."

Verity was probably right. I resumed our stroll. "At least we know what we have to do next."

"Stop in at the bistro?" She nodded to the door of the restaurant.

"No…I was thinking more about visiting the lawyer Walter

mentioned." I pulled up the gallery app on my phone. "Look, he's one of the people Ruby was planning to meet the day after she was killed. Like Walter said, maybe she was going to disinherit a *certain someone*."

Verity scowled. She was doing that noticeably more often.

I matched her face.

"Fine." She dropped a big eye roll. "We can think about that tomorrow. But for now, can we get a sandwich? That ice cream did nothing for me."

I hated to admit she was right, but after Walter coughing up a lung when we caught him off guard, I was inclined to agree. Too bad this was the closest place to get a sandwich, and with my luck, Officer Fancy Pants would be inside fawning over Ella and—

"I see that look on your face." Verity snorted. "It's just a sandwich. Bread, meat, and cheese. Eating here doesn't mean you're relinquishing your one true love into the arms of the enemy."

"I wasn't think—"

Verity challenged me with an eyebrow that tented over her sunglasses. "Stop pretending you don't know what I'm talking about. Besides, Ella usually parks out front, and her car isn't here." She tugged my arm. "Like I said, it's just a sandwich."

"Fine...a sandwich. Whatever." I hiked the strap of my handbag higher on my shoulder and flung open the door to the bistro.

The smell of basil and garlic wafted all the way to the entrance. A sign asking us to take a menu and seat ourselves sat atop the hostess stand. Few customers occupied tables throughout the dining area, leaving us our choice of seating. Verity and I made our way to a booth in the corner near the window.

I perused the menu, noting all the crossed-out items. "There doesn't seem to be much left to choose from."

"But you can't beat the prices." Verity's optimism chafed. "The French dip looks good."

"Next time, we should probably eat dinner before ice cream."

Verity leaned over the table and scrunched her nose. "I don't think there will be a next time here. Pretty sure she's closing shop in a few days."

Boo-hoo.

I mentally kicked myself for the uncharitable thought. Instead, I focused on the menu until my phone buzzed on the table. "Not again." I groaned, unsure whether I wanted to look at the text message or delete it unseen.

Verity swiped it off the table and unlocked it before I could object.

"Hey, wait." I grabbed for it, but she held it out of reach. "How did you know my password?"

"You're not as sneaky as you think. In fact," she said, glancing at my message, "you ought to be a little more careful. Ohhhhh…"

"Wait…can I at least read it?"

She vehemently shook her head. "I don't think that's a good idea."

"But it's *my* message."

"From an ex who treated you abominably." Verity tended to use bigger words when she was miffed.

I slumped against the booth. "James is saying it was a big misunderstanding, and then when I started thinking about it, I realized—"

"That he was lying. Right?"

"Was he, though?" My memories of those last days in LA. were a little hazy after six weeks in Beaver Bluff—time had a way of glossing things over. What did I really know about his relationship with what's-her-name? I fingered the edge of the menu. "What if I overreacted? Maybe what he did wasn't all that bad."

Verity stuffed my phone into her flannel pocket. "I hope you're joking. Didn't you tell me you caught him with someone else?"

"Yes, but I may have not told you the whole truth." Now that I'd been hanging out with Verity, I'd even started trying to be more honest with myself. The whole situation with James was horrible, but he may not have been the only one to blame.

Verity's eyes slivered. "When you told me he replaced you both personally and professionally with a so-called younger version of yourself, what did you leave out?"

What, indeed? There was so much, I didn't quite know where to start. If I was going to get to Verity-level honesty, I needed to come completely clean. I worked the edges of the worn menu harder. "I left out the part that I may have deserved to lose my job, but I was so angry—" Even now, fury simmered inside me. "That I told James I never wanted to see him again."

"Then what happened?" The last of the evening sun slanted into Verity's eyes, but that didn't stop them from bugging out.

I drew a deep breath. "Then a few days later, when I went back to the office to apologize, he was with *her*, and she even kissed him—and he didn't stop her." The image was forever burned in my head. My heart banged harder as I spoke. "What he did wasn't right. That has to be some kind of ethical violation according to the business and whatnot, but it may not have actually been cheating."

Verity's expression morphed from shock to curiosity, then settled somewhere between sadness and sympathy. "There now, doesn't it feel better to get the truth out there?"

In a funny way, it kind of did. Who knew? At least she didn't ask me why I'd lost my job.

She handed my phone back. "It's your decision what you want to do, but remember, even if he didn't technically cheat, he certainly didn't have to move that fast."

A server with a slicked-back ponytail and a goatee sauntered up to the table. "Are you ladies ready to order?"

I took another gander at the menu with slashes through most of the good stuff. "Looks like your menu is thinning out."

"You can say that again." He nodded, glancing between Verity and me. "However, we still have a selection of sandwiches and sides."

"Weird, I thought Ella was still buying supplies." It came out as a question.

The server offered a half-shrug. "I think she's trying really hard to time the stock on hand with our closing date this weekend."

"That's strange because we saw her at the grocery store." Verity studied the server's face. "When was it, KC?"

I snapped my fingers as though trying to remember. "I know —it was the day of the murder."

Verity kicked me under the table. "*Was* it?"

The server grimaced. "The murder was the same day as that gunshot, wasn't it?"

"Yes, there was so much action around here that day." I tried to sound as though I hadn't been in the middle of it.

"I remember because you two came in with the officers shortly after…you know." He cocked his head toward the ice cream shop next door, eyes wide.

"We did." I agreed.

"Ella didn't shop that day. If I recall, I'd asked her to pick up a few things, and she said she had to spend the day in her office closing out accounts." He shrugged. "Said she'd do it the day after."

Which lined up with when we saw her at the grocery store. It also meant she wasn't at the store when the murder happened like she said she was. My pulse skipped, thinking of the possibilities. If she was "in her office" most of that day, she could have easily slipped out the back and murdered Ruby next door. But how would she have known Ruby was there? Still, she had the motive and the opportunity.

The server's expression changed, and he shifted from one foot to the other. "Sorry, I shouldn't really be talking shop with the customers. You came here to eat."

Verity waved him off. "No worries."

"Exactly." I handed him my menu. "I'll have the turkey and avocado sandwich with a side of fries."

He winced. "I forgot to cross the turkey off the menu."

"Okay, I guess I can have it meatless."

The waiter shook his head. "No avocados, either."

"Bread and cheese?"

He looked incredulous. "If that's what you really want."

It wasn't.

Verity chuckled. "Oh, that Ella, out of everything good. I'm going to have to give her a hard time when I see her."

"Right?" The server matched her laugh. "I'm here disappointing customers, and she's out having fun playing bingo."

"Interesting," I said, stuffing my phone inside my handbag. "That's where we're going too."

Chapter Fifteen

BINGO, again.

The gang and I sat in a row at a long table—me, Verity, Naomi, Polly, and Lulu. Noticeably absent was Ella. Apparently, she had an ongoing problem being where she said she would be. Still, I left the seat open next to me, just in case she came in, and I could coax her to the front.

I surreptitiously turned my head every time I heard someone walk into the rec room of the senior center. But so did everyone else, as Walter wasn't there yet, either, and the games couldn't start without the caller.

The smell of cheap coffee filled the air, and against my better judgment, I was already on my second cup of the evening. A sleepless night loomed, but with the amount of work I needed to do for the grand reopening and my new clients—not to mention piecing together whatever I might learn if Ella had the courtesy to actually show up—I needed the caffeine boost. Murmurs rippled through the small crowd the longer we sat waiting.

"Where is he?" The note of concern in Naomi's voice almost made me nervous, too.

"Don't worry, Naomi. I'm sure he'll be here." Verity arranged her bingo cards, then rearranged them with a different one next to her dauber hand. While I wasn't sure about the logic behind shuffling her cards around, it made me want to do the same, just to look like I had a method, too.

Lulu leaned over the table to get a clear view of us. "Did he mention anything about tonight when you saw him at his shop?"

Verity and I both shook our heads. The subject of bingo hadn't come up when we'd sat with him—he'd been too busy revealing secrets about his past life that I was pretty sure Naomi didn't want to hear. The thought of him with Ruby still had me floored.

"Sorry I'm late, folks." Walter ambled into the rec room, all smiles—a big change from his earlier demeanor.

Naomi fanned herself with one of her bingo cards. "We were starting to worry about you."

"I wouldn't miss this for the world." Walter slid on his headset and started setting up the ball cage.

Verity leaned close and whispered. "Look how happy he is now."

"Shouldn't we want our friends to be happy?" I checked my green dauber on the backside of the card to make sure it worked.

"Of course, but you're missing the point." She reshuffled her cards. "Either he's not as bothered by the whole *situation* as he let on earlier, or he's a great actor."

I paused. She wasn't wrong.

What if Walter's innocent schtick was a ruse? After all, I was a pretty bad judge of character. I turned over the events of the day in my head, hoping for a breakthrough, some snippet of information that would blow the case open. What if we were all on the wrong track? Then again, what if the police were, too?

Still, after talking with Walter today, I remembered what a sweet old man he was. And with Naomi currently enamored with him, I hated to think the police would arrest the wrong person, especially once they discovered Walter's financial connections to Ruby.

"Am I late?" A deep voice jerked me out of my thoughts.

Hamson flipped the metal chair next to me around and sat backward, like a guy a decade younger than himself. How lame. Also, a little hot.

I looked him over, top to bottom, noting how his fall-colored flannel brought out the gold flecks in his eyes, even with the poor lighting of the rec room. "What are you doing here?"

Hamson slapped three cards onto the table. "Same thing as you. I feel a lucky streak coming on." He pulled two troll dolls out of his pocket, then whipped their bright hair into a peak before setting them above his cards. As a final touch, he pulled out a picture of his tuxedo cat Figaro and kissed it.

"You've got to be kidding me."

He stopped and met my gaze with a quizzical one of his own. "Got something against my cat?"

"Of course not. It's this whole—" I motioned to his setup. "Plus, you've never been here before."

Hamson aimed his grin at me. "You made it sound like fun."

"Now I *know* you're lying."

Hamson lined his cards up with equal space between them. "Besides that, I really want to win."

"The prizes aren't that great." Although, to be fair, I wanted to win, too. The all-you-can-eat buffet was calling my name.

"If you win—which I doubt—you can give your prize to me." He raised his dark eyebrows suggestively.

"Not a chance." I rearranged my cards again. "How about if I win, I'll let you tag along?"

"Now that sounds like—"

"Shh!" All four of my so-called friends shushed me at once. Verity continued by saying, "Walter's about to get started."

"Welcome everyone, friends, and newcomers." Walter glanced at Hamson, then loosened his collar that was already open. He cleared his throat, making the mic squeal. "Is everyone ready for some b-i-n-g-o?"

A cheer erupted in the room, the loudest from Naomi. Hamson blew on his hands and rubbed them together. He looked like a man who took his bingo seriously, yet something wasn't right. Not by a longshot.

Voices sounded, and more chairs were pulled out behind me. I glanced over my shoulder at the back of the room and saw a few more people settling in. One of them looked oddly familiar, but I couldn't quite place him. Dark hair, clean-shaven, navy trousers. Definitely not a Crumb's customer, but—

"No way." I turned to Hamson, ice in my veins. "You're not here for fun." I lowered my voice. "You brought the state police."

His face turned serious, scarily fast. "I don't know what you're talking about."

"Lying is not a good look on you." I poised my dauber over my cards as Walter called the first number.

"B-seven, b-seven."

Rats.

"Just play." Hamson had two b-sevens.

For the next few calls, we played in silence while I simultaneously worked up my thoughts and held myself back from lashing out at him. Did he think I wouldn't figure out the real reason he was here? On that note, I was still excited he sat right next to me.

"I know exactly why you're here," I whispered between clenched teeth.

Hamson turned to me with a raised eyebrow and a smirk. Without a word, he turned back to his cards and pretended to study them.

"Don't you have better things to do than harass kindly old men?" I was determined to wrangle a confession from him.

Hamson sighed, long and deep.

"B-thirteen, b-thirteen." Walter's face paled every time he looked our way. He even stumbled over his words more than a few times.

Hamson daubed his card. "If you'll notice, I'm not harassing anyone. You're the one not focusing on the game." He reached across and marked my b-thirteen.

I stamped his hand in retaliation. "I can handle my own cards, thank you very much."

"That's debatable."

"What's not debatable is why you're here." I scanned my cards as Walter called the next number. "You should really be looking into your little girlfriend. She's got secrets of her own."

Hamson's hand stopped mid-daub. He squinted at me incredulously. "My little girlfriend?"

"Yeah, you know the one—Ella."

He rolled his eyes so hard his head went with it. "Please tell me you're not still investigating." He air-quoted the last word with his fingers, seeming a lot less worried about me than the last time we had this conversation. Come to think of it, this topic was, apparently, becoming a regular for us.

Ignoring his comment, I pressed ahead, sotto voce. "Did you know she wasn't where she said she was when Ruby was murdered?"

"How is that any of your concern?" Hamson refused to look at me.

"If you weren't so busy making eyes at her, maybe you'd do your job and investigate her alibi. I'm telling you, she had a motive because Ruby drove her out of business, and she had the opportunity. She could have easily slipped next door when the gun went off, and no one was around." The diatribe caused my heart to race, even as I waited for a response.

Hamson drew a lengthy breath, then shook his head. "Man, KC—you just don't know when to stay out of it." And with that, he angled his chair away from me.

Polly leaned forward and grimaced. "What'd you do to tick him off?"

What, indeed?

In trying to help my friend, I'd ticked off Hamson by either shoving my theory forward, or by insinuating he had feelings for Ella.

The sad thing was, he didn't deny it.

DEJECTED and alone was probably overstating how I felt when I left the senior center, but not that far off the mark.

By the time I got home and cuddled Pooh Bear, the sting of Hamson's barely speaking to me the rest of the night started to wear off. It was a good reminder to keep my mouth shut around him. Maybe *I* needed to avoid *him* altogether. Just as well, since I had so many on things to focus on that did not involve falling for Hamson's occasional grin and banter.

I let my dog outside, then I switched on the tablet and got back to work. For every email I'd answered earlier, two more had come in.

Delete, delete, delete.

A message from James beckoned me. Was there any harm in looking? My finger hovered over his name as I waged an internal debate. Maybe I really hadn't given him a fair shot at explaining, and I'd made a big mistake by fleeing LA.

Was my new life in Beaver Bluff a big mistake?

No, especially since I hadn't made anything permanent. Although, life in the slow lane, managing small accounts for friends and neighbors, had a certain appeal. On the other hand, it would be hard to scrap out a real living that way. Maybe I needed to get back to the city sooner rather than later.

I shook off the thought and deleted the message. It didn't matter that I was basically working for free and flying solo—I'd get used to bingo and microwave meals for one, eventually. Aside from the whole murder situation, life was pretty good. I smiled and continued.

Next was Trudi's animal rescue newsletter I'd signed up for to get a feel for how she currently handled communications. The headline featured a pair of sad-looking dogs with eye goobers, and the footer boasted a three-legged cat. This was not the way to woo pet owners—or new donors. I made a note to swing by the ranch in the morning and persuade Trudi not to make any more moves without me.

Melody emailed, asking for copies of the pictures I'd taken for her fall festival. I quickly shot those over to her and added a few more notes to my burgeoning to-do list. It would be a lot easier working with her if I didn't think there was a good chance she'd strangled the life out of Ruby in cold blood. Melody's words in the back office of the sporting goods store spun through my head. There were probably a thousand things she could have meant by her and Rick "going down" together, but murder was the only one that rang true.

By now, my brain hurt. I set the tablet aside and tugged open the front door. With the cool night air blowing in off the ocean, it seemed like a good time to take a walk and organize my thoughts.

Pooh Bear sensed what was about to happen and brought me his leash from his toy basket. I donned a sweater, grabbed my keys, and locked the door behind me. Pooh Bear tugged the leash, so I gave him some slack until he tugged again. In Pooh-code, that meant he wanted to run, not walk. "Not tonight, big guy. You've got to give me a little break." I reeled him back in and purposely slowed my pace. He offered a muted bark in response.

The chilly breeze carried along the smell of pine trees from the forest, backing my rental. Few streetlights lit the neighborhood, which made for better stargazing. At the end of the block, I stopped and inhaled a lungful of fresh air, grateful.

"Let's get home so I can get back to work." Pooh Bear whined as I turned him back around. "Tomorrow, we'll take a long run when I get home."

He looked up at me and smirked. Yeah, I didn't believe me, either. But, somehow, I had to make more time for my best boy.

The quiet street stretched out before us, dark houses lining both sides. Maybe it was later than I'd thought. I patted my pockets but came up empty—my phone was probably at home next to the tablet. Knowing how much work I had ahead, we picked up the pace.

As we approached the house, Pooh Bear sniffed the air, and his fur bristled. A low growl rumbled in his throat. I stopped and listened. Scanned the perimeter. My heart tripped over itself as I waited.

Pooh Bear barked, splitting open the quiet, echoing off the houses. A light turned on across the street.

I froze, unsure what to do. It was probably nothing—an owl or some other critter from the forest. All I saw were shadows and I heard not a whisper of sound besides Pooh and me.

After a few moments, I shook off my nerves and turned up the walkway to the house. "Let's get inside." I pulled out my keys to ready myself for a quick entry.

Pooh's ears stood at attention, and he continued to growl.

I hustled to the front door, fumbled with the key, and finally pushed our way inside. Quickly, I locked it and leaned against the door, catching my breath. Silly, and yet, I couldn't help but feel like I wasn't so alone after all.

Chapter Sixteen

MORNING ROLLED AROUND ENTIRELY TOO FAST.

After working late into the night, I fell asleep—in my clothes, no less—sometime after two. Just a few more days and the grand reopening would be over, and I could resume a somewhat normal schedule, whatever that was.

I pounded down a few coffees, then Pooh Bear and I headed toward Trudi's small ranch. Given how many animals she cared for, I assumed she'd be awake, even though the sun had just cracked the horizon.

The property sat at the edge of town and only occupied a few acres, at most. Evidently, the word "ranch" was used liberally, though there was no shortage of animals, judging by all the noise. Trees bordering the land took on a bright glow in the morning light.

Pooh Bear crooned when I climbed out of the car, as though calling out to long-lost pals. A chorus of dogs responded, along with a few neighing horses. Despite the friendly greetings, it was probably best to leave him in the car, though his expression told me he vehemently disagreed.

A man stood near a corral where dogs ran free, and I headed that direction, picking my way over rough ground. Note to self—

this was no place for heels.

Trudi rounded the corner with a golden-furred puppy in hand. Her work boots and sturdy denim jeans were definitely more appropriate for the setting. "Hey there." She shifted the dog over her shoulder. "We weren't expecting you."

I held up my phone. "It seemed like a good time to stop by and take a few pictures and get familiar with your place." *And stop you from hurting your own cause.*

"Absolutely. Come out to the barn, and we'll get you all set up, KC." She motioned with her head, then led me back the way she'd come. "What does KC stand for, anyway?" The puppy on her shoulder whined in my direction.

"I'll never tell." My ankles wobbled on the uneven ground. "Let's just say there was an unfortunate haunted house incident in grade school, which led to an even more unfortunate play on my name. That's when I switched to KC."

Trudi glanced over her shoulder and smiled. "I'm right there with you. I was teased about my full name mercilessly, too."

I caught up to her and tickled the puppy's chin. "Now I'm curious—what is it?"

She winked. "I'll never tell."

"You got me there." The puppy licked my fingers. "Speaking of names, what's this little fella called?"

Trudi stopped and handed me the pup. "This 'little fella' is actually a girl named Cujo. Her owner went into assisted living a few days ago and couldn't keep her."

"That's not even right to call this love bug Cujo." Reverting to a baby voice only seemed natural while scratching behind Cujo's ears and receiving a sweet nuzzle under my chin. "Why wasn't she in the newsletter you sent out?"

"Well, that's kind of obvious, isn't it?" Trudi peered at me through a curtain of brown bangs. "She's too cute. No one would feel sorry enough to take her home."

I mentally face-palmed myself while staying neutral on the outside. "That's not how this works. People want adorable animals to take home with them." Cujo licked my cheek. And oddly, I wasn't grossed out.

"But then they might not feel the need to help finance the rescue." Trudi rubbed her face and sighed. "And now, with Ruby gone, we're really going to need additional funding."

This one and about a dozen other charities in town.

"After the grand reopening this weekend, you and I can sit down and talk about market segmentation and how we'll need different tactics for different audiences." I Eskimo-kissed Cujo. "In the meantime, let's get some new pictures to promote the adoption day."

Trudi's face brightened. "Great! Let me set you up with one of my volunteers to get started."

I followed Trudi to a building near the barn, jostling the puppy in my arms like a baby. While I was excited to get some decent photos of the animals at the rescue, I was halfway certain I didn't want to take one of Cujo and risk never seeing her again.

AFTER VISITING THE RESCUE, I worked a short counter shift at Crumb's and waited for Verity's lunch break. I texted her to meet me there, and we'd walk to the office of Benson Michaels, Ruby's lawyer. She reluctantly agreed.

"I really don't think you're going to get any information out of the lawyer. They have an attorney-client privilege to abide by." She slid on her sunglasses as we stepped into the alley. "I think you're going down a dead end."

"Or chasing a red herring," Naomi said as she took Pooh Bear's leash from me. "That's what they call them in my cozy mysteries."

"You guys, we have to hunt down every clue we can." I looked between Naomi, Verity, and Polly, who joined the huddle outside the back door. "You saw Hamson last night—he was watching Walter."

Naomi's coral-colored lips quivered. "Maybe he really just wanted to play bingo."

"Yeah," Polly chimed in.

I shook my head. "No one *really* wants to play bingo."

"Hey!" The three of them turned on me.

I held up my hands in surrender. "You know what I mean. Hamson was clearly there for other reasons." The smell of the nearby dumpster turned my stomach.

"And *you* found a way to turn him off." Polly tsked at me. "For all you know, he might've wanted to be there with you. After all, he sat right next to you."

That's what I'd thought at first, too. But his strange reaction when I confronted him about Walter and tried to tell him about Ella proved differently.

Pooh Bear whined at Naomi, who reached down and ruffled his fur. "You girls get going and catch up with us later. I'm going to get this guy some lunch."

Verity and I set off down the alley, in the opposite direction of the town square, until we converged with a side street that led downtown. The sun shone considerably brighter than when I'd been at the ranch, and I peeled off my sweater to enjoy what would probably be the tail end of warm weather before a permanent chill settled over Beaver Bluff. We passed a jewelry store, a pharmacy, and a mini-mart before I spoke.

"Why do you think Hamson was really at bingo?" I quick-stepped to keep up with Verity's long stride.

"Who knows? I'm beginning to think our whole investigation is a wild-goose chase." Her lips pursed with frustration.

"I've thought the same thing." My phone buzzed inside my handbag, but I ignored it. The last thing I needed was more items to add to my to-do list, which is what the call or text surely entailed. "But we have to keep going." I stopped her and forced her to meet my gaze. "Look, I know I've kind of changed my opinion about Walter right now, but let's assume, for the sake of friendship, that someone else killed Ruby. We can't let an innocent old man go to jail. It's just not right."

Verity pushed her sunglasses up the bridge of her nose. "So you think the police are barking up the wrong tree like last time."

"I just don't trust them."

"You can't possibly think Hamson is crooked."

"Crooked? No, of course not." As much as we ruffled each other's feathers last night, I knew there was no straighter arrow than Hamson. He'd proven that the last time there was a murder. "I just think we have everyone's best interests in mind, and the state police may just be trying to mop this up quickly and get back to…wherever it is they came from. Hamson said as much when the whole thing started, and they have way more control of this thing than he does."

Verity started walking again. "Then I guess we really don't have a choice."

The lawyer's office was situated as an anchor in an upscale strip mall to the east of the grocery store. Next to it was a bank and a shoe boutique I had yet to visit. (How had I not seen it before? They definitely needed help with promotions!) The parking lot was filled with BMWs, Porches, and even a Bentley. Nary a clunker in sight. Where had these people been hiding? Beaver Bluff definitely had a side I wasn't aware of—a group of people I needed to get in touch with to build my clientele.

"You can't just waltz in there and ask who stands to win big by Ruby's death." Verity tucked her sunglasses into the pocket of her peach-colored button-down shirt—a nice change from her usual flannel. "We needed to plan this a little better."

"Au contraire." I held up my finger. "We're making an appointment to set up my new business as an LLC, or whatever."

Verity's nose wrinkled. "Do you really need one yet?"

"Maybe," I said defensively. "For all you know, my business could take off."

She rolled her eyes. "Really?"

"Fine. I got the idea when you told me about your patron at

the library, asking about how to set up an LLC. It's a perfect cover."

"Pretty sure Benson Michaels won't see you right this minute. You may not get an appointment with him at all. Anyone who worked with Ruby probably has an exclusive clientele."

"Hey, I'm exclusive." I hiked my *exclusive* handbag up my *exclusive* shoulder.

Verity snorted. "Keep telling yourself that." She whisked open the door to the law office of Benson Michaels and Associates and gestured with flair. "After you, madam."

I smirked and breezed past her.

The inside of the office smelled like money—old money. A large fountain burbled in the corner, and expensive plants filled the lobby. My heels clacked on the marble flooring as we made our way to the reception desk.

"Benson Michaels and Associates, please hold…Benson Michaels and Associates, please hold." The receptionist finished pushing buttons and looked up at us. "How may I help you?" The phone rang again, and the strain around her eyes from not answering it showed.

"I'm here to see Benson."

"Do you have an appointment?" She flinched when the phone rang again.

"Go ahead." I gestured to the blinking light on her desk.

She held up a finger, pressed a button, and flew through two calls lickety-split. "Thank you for waiting." She glanced at the clock. "Almost lunchtime."

"I know the feeling," Verity said.

The receptionist noticed her as if for the first time. "You're the librarian who helped me last week when I needed to do some minor research."

Verity smiled. "That's right. I'd forgotten."

"I appreciate you directing me to the law library. I'm new around here, so I didn't know."

"No problem."

The middle-aged woman relaxed and took a deep breath, noticeably more at ease after identifying her connection with Verity. "I'm really sorry, but appointments have to be made a few weeks in advance."

"Totally understandable." I slid into an easy smile as I scrambled for Plan B—not that I'd assumed plan A was going to work. But really, who knew a law office would be quite this busy? "Let's get me scheduled, then. I'm starting a business, and I need some legal advice."

The woman—whose nameplate read Brenda—frowned. "That's not really the type of law Mr. Michaels specializes in. He's more of an estate, trust, and wills lawyer. Let me get you in with one of his associates."

For the next few minutes, Brenda set up an appointment I had no intention of keeping. Meanwhile, I flashed Verity a look, pleading with her to step in. She offered a mini-shrug and a grimace.

Another lady swept in behind the reception area. "You can head out to lunch now, Bren."

Relief washed over Brenda's face. She handed me an appointment card, then peeled off her headset. "If you have further questions, Meg can assist you."

"No, I think that was it." My thin voice betrayed my disappointment. Verity had been right that this idea, at least, was a wild-goose chase.

Outside, Verity and I slowly descended the steps, and a cool breeze swept over us. For the moment, it seemed our sleuthing hit a wall. I could go talk to Rick at the sporting goods store next, or—

"Do you really think David might be guilty?" Verity's words interrupted my thoughts. She bit her lip, and her eyes cut away from me.

I winced. "Yes, I really do." Saying so made me feel bad since she clearly wanted him to be innocent, but we had to look at all the possibilities.

"If you really think so, then we probably need to make amends with him. I mean, he couldn't have been *that* mad at you."

I thought back to the incident at the salon. "Hopefully not. I mean, he has to understand that we just want to help find out what really happened to his grandmother. If he's innocent, then that shouldn't be a problem."

Just then, Brenda hustled out the door, nearly bumping into us. "Oops, sorry about that. Guess I was in a rush to grab lunch."

Verity perked up. "No worries. By the way, did you ever find what you needed that day I helped you in the library?"

"I did, thank you." Brenda continued toward the parking lot.

Verity followed. "I bet it's been crazy around your office lately."

"Yeah," I piped in, picking up on Verity's cue. "What with the death of your big client."

Brenda stopped and rolled her shoulders. "Which one? There's been a lot happening."

"Our friend Ruby Maxwell." Verity shaded her eyes.

"That's turning into kind of a mess. She told me she was meeting with at least one person she was getting ready to write out of her will, so I don't even know what's going to happen now." Brenda clapped her hand over her mouth. "Oh man, I shouldn't have said anything." She glanced over her shoulder at the office. "You won't mention this, will you?"

"Of course not." I waved her off at the same time I stepped closer. "I'm sure her grandson David wouldn't want that tidbit getting out, either."

Brenda wrinkled her nose. "Why would he care?"

"It was my understanding that he's the one who was getting written out." I shrugged as though it were common knowledge.

"Not that I'm aware of." Brenda stepped back. "Anyway, I'd better go."

When she was gone, Verity pumped her fist. "That puts David back in the clear."

"Not necessarily. He still likely stands to inherit, which is a pretty big motive, and remember, Walter implied that he and Ruby had been having their differences." I started a slow walk back toward the bakery. "It also means that someone else was getting written out, and our suspect pool is bigger than before. We need to see her appointment book to figure out exactly who all Ruby was supposed to meet with." I turned to Verity. "You're right—we need to make things right with David because I'll bet he knows."

Chapter Seventeen

A THOUSAND LEADS TO FOLLOW, and never enough time for more than one.

After our chat with Brenda—thank goodness for the loose-lipped assistant—Verity headed back to the library. I took a detour instead of directly returning to Crumb's since I was only a block from the town square. Rick and Melody's fight still lingered in my thoughts, and I knew there was more information to be gained.

The sporting goods store had a distinctive smell that wafted over me every time I walked inside. A surprising number of customers milled around the entrance and queued at the cash register. Jacob Rhine, the owner of the outdoor adventure company, exited the line with a bag in hand, nearly bumping into me.

"Hey, there. I planned on calling you later today." The imaginary Verity on my shoulder kicked me. But for all she knew, it was true.

Jacob's half-mast eyes opened a little wider when he noticed me. Then he tilted his head and peered closer. "Dude, that's some rad hair."

"Uh…yeah. That's what I was going for." I touched my head self-consciously. "Anyhoo, after looking at your website and social media, I have some ideas I want to run by you—after the grand re-opening at Crumb's this weekend."

"Cool. My schedule should be open by then, too." Jacob held up his big bag. "I have a mountaineering group coming in, and I needed a few extra supplies." He leaned close. "I hate to pay retail, but I was in a bind."

"I hear you. As a business owner, you've got to do what you've got to do." I shrugged in agreement.

Jacob's eyes widened again. "Hey, I'm getting a local mountaineering group started for beginners. Maybe you could join us."

There was nothing I'd like less. I cleared my throat. "Wow, that sounds…super. Super interesting, I mean. Even better, I could help you *promote* it."

"The group was my buddy David's idea." Jacob glanced around and stepped aside to let another shopper pass before he spoke. "It seemed a little weird, so soon after what happened to his grandma Ruby, but whatever."

Weird, indeed. I tried to wrap my mind around what this could mean. "I didn't realize you and David were friends."

"I hang out with a lot of people." Jacob angled toward the door. "Give me a jingle if you want to join the group."

"Sure thing." I turned away from Jacob and scanned the store. In addition to the floppy-haired teen named Ryan, who usually worked, a man with salt-and-pepper locks manned the cash register. He finished with a customer who thanked him by name —Rick.

I loitered near the camping gear, waiting for the rest of the line to dwindle. The shelves held outdoor stoves, coolers, tents, chairs, and other odds and ends like small lights and ropes. Ropes that looked similar to the one that strangled Ruby. Maybe climbing rope and camping rope looked just like ropes used to tow cars and string clotheslines. If only I could have another look at the murder weapon to note the subtle differences.

With so many varieties of rope available in Rick's store, it shoved him and Melody both back to the forefront of my suspect list. And if I could just—

"Checking out the ropes?" Rick stood about three feet from me but occupied most of the aisle with his broad shoulders and barrel chest. The glint in his eyes made it seem like he'd been privy to my exact thoughts. Perhaps I should have devised my plan to talk to him more carefully.

I tried to speak around the knot in my throat. "No…uh…"

"Cat got your tongue?" Rick flashed a grin that took up more space on one side of his face than the other.

"You're Rick, right?" I snapped out of my reverie, determined to do what I came in for. After all, I was a professional. At least I would be when I rustled up a few more clients. I stuck out my hand, which he reluctantly accepted. "I'm KC. I work with your wife…er…soon-to-be-ex-wife."

His features darkened at the mention of Melody. "You're peddling yarn up at the shop?"

"No, no. Nothing like that." If I had a business card, I'd have pulled it out. As it was, I patted my chest. "I work in social media and promotions."

"Wait, I've seen you before. You work in that bakery."

He'd seen me there? Odd, since I'd never noticed him. I really needed to pay more attention to my surroundings.

"I'm at Crumb's part-time. It's my aunt's bakery. In fact," I said as I pulled a flyer from my handbag, "we're having a grand reopening this weekend. You should come."

"Why would I do that?" Rick fisted his hands on his waist without taking the flyer.

"Maybe so you can get ideas for your own store?"

"What's wrong with my store?"

This was not going well.

I riffled through my thoughts and tried to put together a coherent message on the fly. "There's also going to be some great prizes and lots of food. The whole town's going to be there."

He quirked his eyebrows.

"I mean, a lot of people will be there. Maybe not the whole town."

Rick took a step back. "Is there anything I can help you find while you're here? Are you looking to go camping?"

"Actually, after talking to Melody, I was coming to offer you a consultation. Since I'm already working with her, it would be like a two-for-one deal."

"I don't need a consultation."

"Well, that's not what she said." I chuckled, finally feeling my groove. "I mean, she didn't come out and *say* it, but she implied you could use a little help with promotions."

Rick's muscles bulged out of his blue polo shirt as he folded his arms. "Oh, she did, did she? Why, I ought to—"

"Just to benefit your bottom line, of course."

He glanced around, then lasered in on me with slivered eyes. "What else did she say?"

I sifted through my brief interactions with Melody for anything that would be useful. I tapped my finger on my lips. "She mentioned that the two of you are still, shall we say, *stuck together* because of the business. Maybe if you rake in a little more profit, you could get...untangled." I was pretty sure it didn't work that way, but it sounded logical.

Rick rolled his eyes, which was a little unbecoming on a middle-aged man. "I was never looking to get *untangled* from my wife in the first place."

"I'm so sorry. I heard about that, too." I did my best to look bereft.

"What did you hear, exactly?"

I waited for a customer to pass us and round the corner before I whispered. "I heard Ruby told your wife about your...extracurricular activities."

Rick's cheeks reddened. "It wasn't even true."

I offered a slow, measured shrug. "I'm just repeating what Ruby, herself, told me."

His breaths came through his nose in quick snorts as the color in his face deepened. His mouth moved as though he had a few words to share but was forcing himself to hold back.

"I'm not saying it was true." I fingered the rope hanging on the peg. "Ruby told more than her fair share of tales if you know what I mean."

Rick glanced from my face to my fingers and back again. "Wait, are you suggesting…"

I retracted my hand. "I'm not…oh…do you think I think…."

"Look," he said, holding his hands up in a surrender pose. "I didn't have nothing to do with what happened to that old bag."

"Of course you didn't. I mean, you were *here* when Ruby was murdered, right?"

Rick shook his head slightly before seeming to catch himself.

"I seem to recall it happened when everyone ran across the street when that gun went off." I peered around him toward the guy at the cash register. "I'm sure your Melody vouched for you when the police came by, right? Wasn't she supposed to be manning the register?"

"The police didn't come by." Rick enunciated each word with venom.

"They didn't?" I scratched my head. Looked like the Beaver Bluff PD, along with the staties, was blowing it. Again. "I mean…why would they? Just because Ruby broke up your marriage doesn't mean you'd strangle her for it." I accidentally glanced at the rope. "In any case, can I pencil you in for a consultation?"

Rick grimaced, pivoted, then called over his shoulder. "I don't need your help with my store."

"Right, totally understood." I waved the flyer at him. "Don't forget to stop by the grand reopening on Saturday!"

I FINISHED out a quick shift at Crumb's—at least I had a small income, supplemented with pastries—then headed to the library for a quiet place to work. Verity set me up in a study room, where I spread out my notes alongside my tablet.

After designing and sending out e-invitations, securing delivery on the so-called healthy food that I'd promised Griff and Holly for the reopening, and submitting a press release to the Beaver Bugle, I kicked back and scrolled through social media.

The adorable pictures I'd taken at the ranch were up—all in one album, which was *not* what I'd recommended to Trudi. Sadly, only the same three people had liked the pictures. I added myself to their number. The little fluff ball named Cujo had my heart in the palm of her paws.

Jacob had already posted a few pictures from his mountaineering group today. The entire crew looked entirely too ambitious for my taste.

A solo picture of James appeared on my feed, and I quickly scrolled past his smoldering gaze. No need to go there just because he was pestering me three times a day. In fact, it seemed like a good time to stop following him online altogether.

But I didn't.

Instead, I continued to scroll around, looking at my old friends in my old life. The elegant restaurants, glamorous couples, and beachfront houses caused a smidgen of yearning to wriggle inside me. Then came the glitzy clothes, the high-end cars, and the next big event. I'd thought those were my people. Now I was back in Beaver Bluff—hiding, according to James's last text—with zebra hair and bingo.

"You ready to go?" Verity poked her head inside the door.

I sat up. "Is it already time? I barely got started."

She glanced at her watch. "We have to leave now, or we won't get a quick session in before the gang shows up at your place."

"At my place? I don't remember making any plans." I switched off my tablet and slid it inside its case. "Also, I don't remember agreeing to a workout, either."

Verity raised a pointed brow, which meant she was not letting me out of a sparring session at the martial arts studio. Which I dreaded with my whole being. It was one thing to mess around at my house and quite another to spar in public.

"Let's go." She beckoned me with her pointer finger.

"Fine, but I'm still not wearing a gi."

FAMOUS LAST WORDS.

Before I had a chance to accept or deny, Verity had me kitted out in a white gi, ready to tumble. Worse, I had to go barefoot. After years of wearing heels, it felt altogether unnatural. Thankfully, she'd arranged for us to have the studio to ourselves but made no such promise for next time. I promised *myself* that I'd somehow be too busy to go.

"Hee-ya!" Verity's shout caught me off-guard.

"That's a new one." I plugged my ear.

"Try it. It adds some power into your moves." She got into position. "When I come at you, I want you to do a leg sweep and take me down."

Before I could respond, she went into motion, and as if by instinct, I swept her legs from under her. "Hee-ya!" Actually, the shout felt pretty good.

After nearly an hour, we finished.

"You're getting a lot better." Verity's perky voice did nothing to soothe my aching muscles, or the bruise I was pretty sure was blooming on my bottom from a particularly brutal fall.

"I'm not sure it'll do any good." I waved at the owner of the martial arts studio as he locked the door behind us.

Verity clicked her key fob. "It sure helped you when you were in trouble last month. And for all you know, you could find yourself in another dangerous position. You can't be too careful."

"Whatevs." I was too tired to shrug. "Do we have to have a meeting with the gang tonight?"

Verity stopped, grabbed my shoulders, and shook me. "Are you even hearing yourself?"

"Vaguely."

"We have more clues to fill everyone in on after talking to Brenda today."

"And Rick." I ceded the point.

"Plus, I have pushpins so we can fix up our crime board."

"Fine. But is anyone bringing food?" My stomach growled. As much as I hated to admit it, I probably needed a vegetable or two.

"Duh." Verity climbed inside her car. "I'll see you there."

Minutes later, we rounded the corner into my subdivision on the edge of town. Already, darkness had settled over the forest, and the moon cast an eerie glow. Verity parked at the curb, and I pulled into the driveway. The others had yet to arrive.

When I switched off the engine, I heard barking. Not Pooh Bear's playful barking or conversational barking, but barking that was dark and alert. I climbed out, sharing a glance across the front yard with Verity. We both looked around, and Verity turned on the flashlight of her phone. I did the same, casting the beam to the far side of the driveway and toward the bushes under the front window.

We met at the walkway that led to the door.

"What's going on?" She stage-whispered loudly enough for the neighbors to hear—neighbors who were now turning on their lights.

"I don't know. Something must've just happened." I looked at her, then followed her line of sight to the door.

The door where a giant knife protruded from a note pinned underneath.

Chapter Eighteen

THE BACK of my neck prickled, and adrenaline pounded through my veins.

Verity and I shared a frozen glance as Pooh Bear continued barking in the backyard. Whoever had stuck the note to the door had to have been here in the last few minutes.

Was maybe even still around.

"What do we do?" I whispered.

Verity's expression turned hard. "They wouldn't dare be hanging around." Her body shifted into a fighting stance.

I dusted off the front of my dress. "You're right. No one would be foolish enough to be here now that we're back." The bravado in my voice was a total farce. But with Verity at my side, we could overpower whoever was dumb enough to still be here after knifing a note to my door.

Verity's head pivoted as she took in her surroundings. Then, slowly, she straightened and moved up the walkway. "We should be safe."

I tagged along behind Verity, determined to take the self-defense stuff more seriously, as Verity had urged me less than ten minutes ago. Despite her confidence, which would have to be enough for the both of us, my heart still felt like putty. At least Pooh Bear's barks were subsiding.

Two cars pulled up—Polly's enormous Lincoln Town Car and Lulu's Volvo.

"Oh, no. We can't let them see this." I hurried past Verity to the front door.

"We don't even know what it says yet. Hurry, read it." Verity pointed.

I reached for the note but stopped. "What if there are prints on there? Maybe I shouldn't touch it."

"The gang might get suspicious when they see the knife sticking out of your door." Verity's eyes saucered. She shined her flashlight onto the note.

The red marker stood in contrast to the plain, college-ruled paper. I leaned close and read aloud. "Back off, or one of your friends is next." I covered my mouth to keep from gasping.

The ladies ambled out of their cars and started gabbing curbside.

"Yoo-hoo. We're here," Naomi called over Pooh's occasional barks.

"Do you have to announce it to the whole world?" Polly asked.

A window across the street opened, and Krystal's voice added to the noise. "What's going on? Did something happen to Pooh Bear?"

I startled. *Had* something happened to Pooh Bear? No, only an idiot would go after him. His bark was angry, not wounded. I needed to get to him, but I also needed to handle the door situation.

"What's going on up there?" Lulu locked her car and started toward us.

I spun around, blocking the note with my body. "Nothing."

"We just finished our workout and came here," Verity stuttered.

Polly's smirk was clear, even in the scant moonlight. "What

does that have to do with what you're covering up?" Her finger moved in a swirly motion, aimed at us.

"Us, cover something?" I gestured to my chest, then looked up at Verity. "Does that seem like something we would do?"

Verity winced.

"All right, out with it." Lulu joined Polly and Naomi, a formidable trio.

Verity and I reluctantly parted to reveal the note. Naomi and Lulu gasped. Polly released a string of threats that would make a henchman lose his bowels. After the three of them read it, they each had conflicting thoughts on what to do next, ranging from calling the police to hunting down the perp and beating him senseless with his own body parts. Frankly, neither of those options appealed.

"If we call the police, they're going to know we've been investigating the murder," I reasoned. "Hamson already told me that those guys from the state don't mess around, and I don't really want to test them."

"But if we don't call the police, then we're leaving *your friends* vulnerable," Verity emphasized the words on the note as she gestured to the group. "While I'm not worried about myself, I'm concerned about everyone else."

"Hey." Polly's eyes lit with fire as she shook her fist. "That scum better not try anything with me."

The sound of footsteps crossing the road caused us all to stop talking, and even Pooh Bear had ended his rant in the backyard. Krystal picked up her pace when she caught us staring in her direction. The gang and I slid together to cover the door.

"Don't stop talking on account of me." Krystal pinched the front of her bathrobe closed and glanced over her shoulder at Clyde, who was peering out their window. "What's going on? Why was Pooh Bear barking?"

"Uh, nice night for a walk." Lulu clearly wasn't cut out for undercover ops.

"Just get a load of that fresh air." Neither was Naomi, who

sniffed as though inhaling the scent of sunshine and roses.

Krystal grimaced. "You guys are so not sneaky. Look, if there's something happening in the neighborhood, I'd kind of like to know about it."

Good point, plus she might have noticed something. "Verity and I got here a few minutes ago and found this." I ushered the gang aside to reveal the threat.

Krystal stepped up to the door and leaned close to read the note, visible with the beam of light from Verity's phone. "Oof. What are you going to do?"

Ignoring her question, I launched into one of my own. "Did you see anything? We figured this only happened right before we got here since Pooh Bear was still barking." Thankfully, his angry barking had stopped, and now he was crooning for attention.

"Despite what some of you may think, Clyde and I don't sit and watch the neighborhood." Regardless of her light tone, Krystal's words hearkened back to the last murder when I'd seen them watching from the window and grilled them about it. "Also, if I'd seen this happen, I would have called you."

"I appreciate that." A backward glance at the note sent another shiver down my spine. Whatever scumbag wrote it knew how to get to me—through my friends. I pulled the house key out of my pocket. "I'm going to check on Pooh Bear."

"Keep me posted. It's kind of scary that this is happening in our neighborhood." Krystal said goodbye to the gang and made her way down the path, her head turning both ways to scan the area.

Once she was safely inside her house, we resumed our discussion as we made our way inside mine.

"We should call the police." The concern in Lulu's voice haunted me as I went to let Pooh Bear in.

"I don't think that would do a bit of good." Even Polly sounded nervous. "On the other hand, we should probably get this incident on record."

Maybe it *was* best if we called the police, and I took my lumps now. The staties, as Hamson called them, would hound me—maybe even bring charges against me for obstruction—to get me to back off.

Which was precisely what the person who left the note wanted. That also meant I was on the right track. Too bad I didn't know which track it was or where it led. The bottom line was, I had to keep my aunt and my friends safe since the Ice Cream Killer was still on the loose…and had us in their crosshairs.

IT TOOK mere moments for the gang to decide to band together under one roof until the murderer was caught. It took a lot longer to decide whether or not to call the police.

"What are they going to do besides send KC up the river?" The airbed shifted as Naomi situated herself against a mountain of pillows. "I'll tell you—absolutely nothing."

Blankets, suitcases, cots, and snacks packed my living room wall-to-wall. Despite telling the ladies to keep it simple as we traveled to each house gathering items, they transformed my place into slumber party central. At least I knew they were all safe. No way would the killer waltz into this mess. I wasn't entirely sure *I* wanted to be in this mess.

Nevertheless, my place was the best option, given the fact I had the most room and all of Pooh Bear's belongings. He was happy to have company. He meandered between all the ladies, gladly accepting treats and offering happy nuzzles in return. Even though I'd known the person who'd left the note wasn't stupid enough to mess with him, I was still relieved that my pooch was unharmed, and I promised to keep him with me as much as possible rather than leaving him home.

"I still think the police could provide some protection instead of leaving us out here like sitting ducks." Lulu, the only one of the older ladies who refused to pay for a professional pedicure, applied the last of the topcoat to her toes.

"With the way they're so shorthanded?" Polly shook her head. "Not likely. If they had enough resources to protect us, they'd also have enough to find the killer—which they don't. There's no way they'd make it a priority to figure out who left the note."

We all mumbled our agreement, including Pooh Bear.

"I think they mean well." Verity hopped onto the couch and crossed her legs, tucking her feet beneath her. "But they haven't proven they can handle bigger cases." She reached out and touched my knee. "Except for *you-know-who*, of course."

"Who…" I waved my hands in front of me, refuting her thought. "No, no, no. Let's not go there." It was time for me to take control and redirect our conversation, or we'd start having a pillow fight and talking about boys. I pushed off the couch and wended my way around the airbeds and cots until I stood next to the crime board. "Let's go over what we know, then Verity and I can catch you up on what we learned today."

Naomi leaned forward and scanned the board. "I've got to be honest—we're not making much progress. I thought we'd have more clues by now."

There was no use pointing out that if some of us had been investigating rather than getting manicures and playing bingo, we might be further along. To be fair, my attention had been divided, too, between starting my business and preparing for the grand reopening.

Lulu gestured to the knife and note, currently on the coffee table, pushed to the side of the room. "Well, we've got one whopper of a clue now."

Polly snorted. "I'd like to see you pin that to the crime board."

"No one else touches the knife or the note." Verity held up her hands as though fending us off. "We have to keep it exactly as is to preserve the evidence." It was a little hard to take her seriously with the mud mask on.

Naomi scratched Pooh Bear behind the ears. "If none of us had touched it, it'd still be stuck to the door."

Verity, who for some unknown reason kept actual gloves in her glove box, had removed the offending pieces from the door rather indelicately. I was pretty sure that wasn't how crime scene investigations were supposed to work, and that we should have left it alone until daylight when we could do it properly, but I was outvoted. Apparently, our little village was going to be a democracy.

"You know what I mean. We can't touch either piece of evidence from *now on*." Verity's green eyes went wide. "Right now, it's the best clue we have, so we have to be careful."

"You mean more careful than when you yanked it out of the door and dropped it on the ground?" Lulu asked.

"It was wedged in tight," Verity insisted.

"Yeah, but when you tore the paper, that didn't help." Naomi shook her head dolefully.

"You guys," I said, trying once again to redirect, "we have to work with what we have. There's no use rehashing what we could have or should have done."

Polly gestured to the evidence. "How will we examine the knife and paper for more clues if we can't even touch them?"

"I brought this." Naomi reached inside her brassier and pulled out a tiny magnifying glass.

The group oohed, and Polly pointed at her. "Now that's some good preparation, right there."

"I read about it in one of my cozy mysteries." Naomi nodded knowingly.

Everyone hoisted themselves off their cots and airbeds and made their way to the coffee table. Pooh Bear offered a disgruntled snort, now that he was no longer the center of attention. I flipped on the adjacent light in the hallway, then used the flashlight on my phone to get a better look.

"This seems different from other knives I've used." I peered closely at the black handle made from extra grippy material. "Seems a little short for cutting steak and whatnot."

"Oh, honey. This isn't a kitchen knife." Lulu shook her head slightly. "This one is made for the outdoors."

Chapter Nineteen

"OUTDOOR KNIFE?" Who knew there was such a thing? I loomed over Naomi's magnifying glass to get a better look at the rubber grip and sharp edges on both sides of the blade, unlike a cooking knife.

Polly slipped on her readers and started pointing out features. "It's a beauty. See there, it's got the hand guard, appears to be a four-and-a-half-inch blade, give or take. Stainless steel, durable, good for easy access in those dicey situations."

We all gaped at our friend.

She offered an exaggerated shrug. "What? So I know a thing or two. Don't look so surprised."

"Why didn't you tell us all that in the first place? If you know something, you need to share it." Lulu leaned back and fisted her hands on her hips, giving Polly the same look she'd given me as an errant teen.

Polly waved off the comment and went back to studying the clues. "Looks a bit older. No one would leave a knife like this stuck in a door if it were in pristine condition."

"What's it generally used for?" I asked.

"Any number of things, really." Polly peeled off her reading glasses.

"It makes me think Rick or Melody—or both—should be at the top of our list. This is probably the exact type of thing they sell at the store." I racked my brain, trying to remember if knives had been part of the camping display. "In any case, it falls right in line with his behavior toward me today."

"Hold that thought until we finish examining these." Lulu gestured to the knife and the note. "Anyone have thoughts on the paper?"

Verity hovered over the coffee table. "Simple college-ruled page, torn from a notebook. Doesn't look like anything special to me. You can literally find these anywhere."

"But the handwriting," I said, trying to hog in on Naomi's magnifying glass. "It looks so stark and angry with all capital letters."

"Someone sure used a fat marker." Naomi looked up at us without taking the magnifying glass away from her face, giving her one enormous eye. "The red indicates anger, as well."

"Even with all capitals, it's fairly sloppy." Polly nodded around the room. "Definitely the work of a man."

"You can't give penmanship a gender," Lulu argued.

Polly harrumphed. "Tell that to the handwriting experts."

A thoughtful expression crossed Verity's face. "I'm positive Lulu is right, but I can do some checking at the library tomorrow. We don't want to make assumptions based on unverified information."

Polly resumed her appraisal. "Like Naomi said, the perp used a fat marker, red, and from the smell of it, one of the plain kinds, not the kiddie ones that smell like fruit."

"Oh, I like those," Naomi said. "My favorite was always grape. I could sniff those for hours."

"Can I tell you all about Rick now?" I was pretty sure we'd gleaned all the information we could from the note and knife—at least without the ability to lift fingerprints.

The group agreed as they made their way back to their respective airbeds and cots. Pooh Bear started hinting for snacks from each of the ladies. Since I still hadn't eaten after the workout with Verity, I followed his lead. Instead of launching into what we'd learned today, I headed for the kitchen with nary an argument from my friends.

Though I wasn't a whiz at baking or putting together gourmet meals—or anything remotely healthy, for that matter—I could set up a charcuterie board with the best of them. White cheddar, sharp cheddar, and provolone cheeses, along with salami, ham, and turkey, made up the bulk of the spread. I added two different types of olives, along with crackers and dip.

"Oh, yeah. I was getting hungry." Naomi rubbed her palms together when we gathered at the kitchen table.

Lulu handed out little plates and napkins. "This would have been a better option to take to David's house, rather than a tub of potato salad. I *knew* you knew better."

"I was in a rush that day," I said defensively. "Besides, it's a little hard to transport a board."

Each of us made our selections, then sat around the table and chatted. The conversation steered away from the investigation, but I was too exhausted from the emotional toll of finding the threat that I didn't mind. Focusing on the sharpness of the cheese was a good distraction.

"Well, at least we can assume Walter didn't do it." Naomi brought us back on track. "He's just too sweet."

"We can't rule anyone out just yet." Verity threw me a nervous glance.

My heart slid down my spine. We hadn't told the gang about Walter's financial involvement with Ruby—I was hoping we'd never have to. If only the killer had already been caught, we could've kept the information to ourselves. But like Lulu said, we all had to share what we knew if we were going to make any progress.

I cleared my throat and shifted in my seat. "This may have nothing whatsoever to do with Ruby's murder...." I waited a beat, trying to gather my courage. I could keep the information to myself because the odds were still against Walter being involved. On the other hand—

"Well?" Polly prodded.

"It's like this." I picked up a napkin and worked it between my fingers, stalling. "Verity and I found out—"

"Mostly, it was KC." Verity gripped Naomi's forearm.

I scrunched my nose at her. "To make a long story short, Walter and Ruby used to be an item. She still had her sights set on him, and when his business was struggling, she offered to help. Ruby was financially involved in the ice cream shop and the lease for the space, and with her gone, all the control reverts back to Walter."

The room fell silent. Stunned looks around the table caused me to hold my breath, waiting for their reaction. I snuck a peek at Naomi. Her wide eyes betrayed no emotion, which meant she was taking it worse than I thought, considering her usual level of expression.

"Whoa, now *that's* a motive." Polly blinked slowly as if taking extra time to absorb the news.

"I had no idea." Lulu clasped her cheeks. "They were together-together?"

Verity chortled. "Almost married."

Polly slapped the table. "That's it. He's back on the list. There are no two ways about it. I always knew he was too good to be true. There's always been something just a little bit fishy about that man, going around snapping his suspenders at unsuspecting women."

"Hey!" Naomi's shout caused Pooh Bear to jump to attention. "Walter is our friend. The whole reason we're investigating the murder is to clear his name. Where's your loyalty?"

"But if he's guilty…." Polly's eyes went wide.

"It's important to have *all* the information," Lulu argued.

"And *you!*" Naomi pointed at me with a shaky finger. Even her white hair trembled. "You were supposed to help us. Now you're throwing shade on my man."

Shade, seriously?

I waved my hands in front of me. "Wait, wait, wait. No one is throwing *shade*. I even said it might not have anything to do with the investigation, remember?"

"You did say that." Lulu rubbed my arm.

"Think about it. If we know this about Walter's financial involvement with Ruby, the cops will know about it soon enough, too." Although, they didn't seem to be keeping pace with us since they hadn't talked to Rick either, or possibly even Ruby's lawyer, to find out who else had a financial motive. What were the state police even doing?

Lulu turned to Naomi. "It really is better if we know all the facts, right?"

Naomi grimaced at me and folded her arms. "I suppose." Then she muttered a few words she must've learned from Polly.

"Lulu's right. It's better for us to know all the information than to be caught off guard. It doesn't mean we think less of Walter. He's our friend," Verity said calmly.

Polly gave each of us at the table a quizzical look. "Is anyone going to mention the fact Naomi called Walter her man?"

We all zeroed in on Naomi. Her expression shifted from accusatory to startled, then settled on sheepish. She patted her chest. "I said that?"

"Pretty sure you did," Verity said.

"Didn't mean anything by it. A simple slip of the tongue." She gestured to the crime board. "Shouldn't we be working on this?" Naomi turned to me. "What happened today with Rick at the sporting goods store?"

"Let's back up and start with Brenda." Verity sat taller and folded her hands on the table, effectively taking control of the sleepover meeting.

"Who's Brenda?" Lulu asked.

"She's the administrative assistant for Ruby's lawyer." The gang resumed their peaceful snacking while Verity spoke. "She accidentally confirmed that Ruby was supposed to meet with someone before she wrote them out of her will. KC and I think that whoever she was writing out killed her before she could legally make that happen."

"That puts David back at the top of the list." Polly was sure eager to pin the blame.

"It doesn't, though." I set my plate aside, knowing all the cheese I'd consumed wasn't doing me any favors. "Brenda also let it slip that the person being written out wasn't David."

Naomi scoffed. "Doesn't she know about attorney-client privilege?"

"Thank goodness for us, she isn't the attorney and isn't bound by that. Or if she is, she doesn't know it," I said.

"Also, I think she's new." Verity was nice to give Brenda the benefit of the doubt.

"So, who was Ruby supposed to meet with?" Lulu asked. "Not that *that* would make them guilty, per se."

"True, but if we could find out who that person is and then establish their whereabouts when the murder happened, it could lead us to the killer." My mind whirred with possibilities.

Verity stood and went to the crime board. She pulled out a marker and wrote *see appointment book* in bold letters.

"Then there was Rick." My muscles tightened as I remembered his angry reaction to my questions. He could easily have slipped next door and murdered Ruby in a fit of rage and could also have knifed the note to my door. I drew a deep breath. "I took a chance and mentioned Ruby's involvement in his divorce from Melody."

"Atta girl," Polly said.

"You came right out and asked that?" Lulu looked horrified.

"That wasn't what I *led* with. Give me a little credit." I resisted the temptation to pout. "Anyway, he was furious that I asked and also defensive when he thought I was tying him to the murder."

Verity sat at the table again. "That seems like a natural reaction. Anyone would be mad."

"But the thing is," I continued as I leaned in, "he didn't have an explanation for where he was when the murder happened."

Lulu bit her lip. "Just because he didn't have an explanation doesn't mean there wasn't one. It just means he didn't feel like telling you."

"But between that, his motive for hating Ruby, and the outdoor knife…." I gestured to the specimen on the nearby coffee table. "It all fits."

Verity uncapped her pen. "So, how do we pursue this lead? We have to take every clue to its logical end until we either establish an alibi for the person associated with the clue, or we find the killer. It's the only way we're going to figure this out."

We all sat in silence, aside from the sound of Pooh Bear chewing his squeaky toy in the corner. What else could we do to establish Rick's whereabouts?

Finally, Lulu spoke. "Didn't you talk to the person who was working that day about Melody?"

"Yeah, and he confirmed she wasn't watching the counter like she said she would be when he returned to the store after the gunshot." It would sure help if people were where they said they'd been when the murder took place.

"Did you ask him about Rick?" Lulu sipped her tea without taking her eyes from me.

"Well…now that you mention it…no."

"Amateur move." Polly shook her head.

"Hey, at least I'm out there trying," I shot back. "Plus, I've been a little busy. In case you all forgot, we have a grand reopening happening the day after tomorrow."

Lulu made a calming gesture with her hands. "Maybe one of us could try asking around."

"I want to do it." Naomi raised her hand. "I can be really sneaky."

I doubted that, but at this point, what did we have to lose? Apparently, none of us were good at keeping a very low profile.

Just then, Verity's phone chirped. She reached inside her

pocket and pulled it out, frowning thoughtfully as she read. Then her eyebrows lifted. "This is unexpected."

"Who is it? What's it say?" I asked as we all perked up.

Verity offered an unsure smile as her thumb hovered over her phone. "It's David, wanting to know if we can get together."

Chapter Twenty

POLLY SHOT out of her chair to take a peek at Verity's text. Lulu and Naomi followed while I brought up the rear.

Despite the connection Verity seemed to feel with David at his house, this still seemed like outside-of-the-box behavior. First, mountaineering, and now this? He hadn't even buried his dear old Grandma Ruby yet.

We all huddled together between the kitchen and living room, trying to read David's message.

"Get together? What do you mean, like a date?" Naomi reached out and grabbed the phone from a startled Verity before reading aloud. "Hey there, it's David. I'm chilling at home with a few people tomorrow night. Want to stop by? Six o'clock."

"But his grandma isn't even in the ground yet," Polly said, echoing my thoughts.

Lulu patted her chest. "I know she was a little…difficult…but how can he…."

Verity snatched her phone back. "Everyone grieves in their own way. Maybe David just doesn't want to be alone during such a hard time."

"That's true, especially in that big house of theirs." Naomi rubbed Verity's back. "He's probably having a terrible time getting used to it."

"I still think having a get-together is in very poor taste," Lulu said.

Polly leaned over and studied the phone. "How did he even get your number?"

"It's not hard," Verity said. "You can find just about anything online or in a database if you have access." She bit her lip as she gazed at the text. "What should I tell him?"

"Yes!" we all said in unison. Pooh Bear grumbled in the background, then went back to his squeaky toy.

"Think about the investigation." I elaborated further. "We need to see what else we can find out from him. Just tell David that we'll be there and ask if we can bring anything."

Polly groaned while gesturing at me. "He didn't invite *you*. You can't just tag along with a tub of potato salad and think you'll be welcomed."

"She's right." Naomi nodded, then Lulu agreed.

"Okay, that stings a little." I stepped back and leaned against the kitchen counter. "But how is Verity going to gather clues without me?"

Verity's eyes slivered, and she stood tall, looming over me. Even with the mud mask, she looked pretty tough. "You're not the only one who knows how to investigate. I can find things out, too."

I placed my hands in a prayerful position. "How do I put this delicately…."

The gang leaned in.

"Unlike you, I don't mind stretching the truth a little to get information," I finished.

"You mean lying? Because I can still get information while telling the truth." Verity fisted her hands on her hips. And while I knew she could, in fact, find information with total honesty, this situation felt different. It required a different skill set.

"So, you're going to march up and tell him you want to know who Ruby might've wanted to cut out of her will? What if something goes wrong? Who'll be there to help? I still think I should go." Plus, I didn't want to miss any of the action. Not that I was going to admit that part.

"The fact remains—you weren't invited," Verity said, folding her arms smugly.

"I have an idea." Naomi's eyes brightened, and her voice took on a mysterious quality. "I read in one of my cozies where the hero and the sidekick used a Bluetooth earpiece, so they could stay in communication, secretly."

We all paused, weighing the option. It could work with Verity inside David's house, and me somewhere close by. It wouldn't be the same as questioning him myself, but we could still make it work.

Lulu issued a weary sigh as she plonked onto a chair. "I don't like the idea of Verity going to David's at all, given the fact he's under suspicion for murder. That said, as much as I hate to admit it, it would be safer with KC there, too."

Everyone looked at each other as if seeking approval for Verity and me to enter a potentially dangerous situation. Finally, there were nods all around.

That settled it—tomorrow night, we were heading back to Ruby's mansion to figure this thing out once and for all.

THE HARD PART about living with a baker is the early hours. The next morning was no exception. Lulu was the first one up and ready to go before four o'clock, and since none of us were supposed to go anywhere alone after the threat, I was up, too.

After quickly donning my new aquamarine leggings and matching tank, I met Lulu in the living room, where we tiptoed around the gang on their airbeds and cots. Naomi lightly snored, and Polly mumbled in her sleep. Pooh Bear opened one eye to acknowledge us before nestling back into his favorite blanket.

Lulu and I arrived at Crumb's shortly after four, where Krystal was already inside working. Had I known she was scheduled for the early shift, I'd have sent my aunt with her. But since I was already at the bakery, I planted myself at a table while the coffee brewed and then started scrolling around my phone.

Sure enough, David had posted several pictures over the last few days on a public profile. Boating, hiking, and laying by the pool. Did he have any clue how callous these photos made him look? Did he care? I scrolled back further, noting how few pictures he'd posted prior to Ruby's death, other than the occasional formal function. To be fair, he was probably enjoying his newfound freedom, not that I would say as much to the gang. I had to agree with Lulu, though, that he was showing poor taste so soon after his grandmother's murder.

But did that make him a killer? Poor taste, in itself, didn't equal guilt, but it sure increased my suspicion. Maybe he'd had enough of being at Ruby's beck and call and then snapped before the person Ruby was supposed to meet that day showed up. Obviously, he'd lied about getting his hair cut when she was murdered. So, where *had* he been? I made a note for Verity to try to work that into the conversation this evening.

I scrolled around a bit more to check on all my new clients and made notes about which other local businesses to contact once life settled down. With the grand reopening happening tomorrow, I scheduled a few more posts advertising the prizes and sent one more press release to the Beaver Bugle.

Finally, the caffeine kicked in. Since it was almost six o'clock, I shot Griff a quick text and asked for a last-minute session at the gym. As much as I hated his brutal training, it was less taxing than working out with Verity. My tender backside was proof. I was almost sorry when Griff immediately texted back that he was available, but I packed up my tablet and made my way to the back door.

"What do you think you're doing? You can't just go trouncing off to the gym." Lulu blocked the doorway and motioned Krystal to abandon her mixer and stand by her side. "We all made a deal —no one goes anywhere alone."

"No killer is ambitious enough to come after me before the sun comes up." I gestured to the dark alley.

She face-palmed herself. "That's not how that works."

"Then walk me to my car, and the next time I'm out of my car, I'll be in public, at the gym," I reasoned. "Since it's still dark, I can see headlights if someone is following me, and I'll drive straight to the police station."

Krystal glanced at Lulu. "She's not wrong. She'd know if someone were tailing her."

Lulu's shoulders drooped with defeat. "Do you promise me you'll stay inside your car if you see headlights?"

"One-hundred percent." I gave her a tight hug. "Believe me, if I can find a good excuse not to work out, I will." That seemed to mollify my aunt, which said a lot about my lack of commitment to fitness, which was apparent to everyone. In a way, it was a lot less stressful than obsessing over my body image, the way I had in LA. I could live with that.

With both Lulu and Krystal watching me walk five yards to my car, I felt pretty safe. Less than fifteen minutes later, I was working out with Griff and regretting all my life's choices, especially the one that led me to the gym before daylight. Twenty-five minutes into the session, I was hating life altogether.

Griff clapped his hands over the sound of weights clanking in the background. "Come on, cupcake. Let's hammer out those reps."

"I'm pretty sure you can't call me that." I snarled, not caring if the other people starting to populate the weight room overheard.

"That's good—channel that anger right into your arms." He clapped again. "Feel the *burn*."

"I'll show you what a—"

"Two more...one more. Okay, that's it." Griff flashed a

million-dollar smile that was entirely too bright for this time of the morning. "Let's cool down."

For the next few minutes, we chatted as I tried to let my body recover. As usual, I liked him a lot more at the end of the session, despite the fact my arms felt like noodles. I spoke to his reflection in the mirror rather than looking eye-to-eye. "You and Holly are still planning to come to Crumb's for the reopening tomorrow, right?"

He nodded appreciatively. "Wouldn't miss it. I've seen some of the prizes you're advertising."

Excellent. It was good to know my message was getting out there. "I saw Holly recently. Looks like you guys are getting all ready for the wedding."

Griff's eyes took on a dreamy quality. "I'm the luckiest man alive. I'm hoping one day she can quit the whole property management gig, and then we can get out and see the world."

That reminded me—I needed to get the door fixed on the rental before Holly found out. I'd have a hard time explaining away the giant gash as normal wear and tear.

A chill slithered over me, remembering last night. Maybe I shouldn't have taken a risk by coming to the gym alone—not that anyone else from the gang would have come with me this early. But the threat was not to be taken lightly. From now on, I needed to stay with my posse, or at least have Pooh Bear at my side when I left the house.

The sun peeked through the windows of the gym by the time I parted ways with Griff. I wiped the sweat from my face and then made my way to the lobby. There was just enough time to swing back to the house and shower before I needed to start my shift at Crumb's. I waved goodbye to the person manning the desk and hello to a few of the regulars I was starting to recognize.

Then the automatic doors whisked open, and Hamson strutted inside.

I halted, as did he. What could I say to him after the bingo blowout? "About the other night." I glanced around, then stepped back slightly so the doors would stop closing halfway, then opening again when they sensed Hamson's frame. A frame that was solid and nicely filled out a wick-away shirt that stretched tautly across his chest—

"Yes?" He prodded.

I shook myself out of the early morning stupor. "I'm really sorry."

"For?" Hamson wasn't going to let me off easy.

"For implying that you weren't doing your job because you're interested in Ella." Her name soured on my tongue. Not that I was jealous…just concerned for the citizens of Beaver Bluff, with a killer still on the loose.

Hamson's eyes roved the lobby before he spoke. "I don't even know where you got that impression."

"Probably because there are so many clues you've missed." I bit my lip to keep from saying more, knowing full well there was a huge clue I was holding back that could get me into big trouble. There was no way I could tell him about the note and the knife.

"I'm not talking about my job, even though that's concerning." His expression softened, and he lowered his voice. "I meant about Ella and me."

I fingered the strap of my workout bag. "Just, you know, seeing that you're at the bistro all the time and not at Crumb's very often anymore."

Hamson's dark eyes sparkled in the early light. "Is that where you want me to be?"

"I…well…no, I mean I don't know." My voice trembled as the gap between us closed, and a rugged scent wafted off him. "You can eat wherever you want."

He leaned in, oblivious to the other two women in the lobby watching him closely. "But when I do eat somewhere else, you seem to come up with crazy ideas and accuse me of not doing my job."

"You know what's crazy? A man who showers before working

out." My rampant thoughts betrayed me before I could censor myself. I looked away before my eyes could say the rest.

Hamson grinned, his dimples deepening. "Well, you never know who you're going to run into at the gym."

"I've never seen you here before."

"That doesn't mean I haven't seen you."

"You have?" I grasped the strap of my bag, now with both hands.

"About every third day." He scoffed. "Your schedule isn't that hard to figure out. You come here after having a few too many sweets, and you start to feel guilty."

I hated how he had me pegged. "Maybe, maybe not."

"You know I'm right." He flashed a smile and started to walk past me. "See, I'm good at detecting." And with that, he breezed away, leaving more than one open-mouthed woman in his wake.

After a deep breath, I walked toward the door and paused while it opened. Fresh morning air greeted me, but Hamson's scent still lingered as I walked toward my car. Had he really noticed me at the gym? Again, my observational skills were a bit lacking.

I pawed around my bag for my keys, even though my car usually unlocked when I got right next to it. It was still a bit dark, so I opened my bag wider the closer I got to the car. The parking lot had filled up quite a bit since I'd arrived. That was the good thing about coming early—not fighting for a spot.

Did Hamson always come this early? Not that I was going to try to see him at the gym on purpose. Sweat might be a good look on him, but on me, it was a different story.

Finally, I dug out my keys as I neared the car. I was almost to the driver's side when I heard footsteps approach quickly from behind. My heart quickened as I remembered my promise to Lulu. I took another step, then a blinding pain smashed the back of my head.

And the world went black.

Chapter Twenty-One

"The police said she fell forward and landed on her face."

Despite the voices blending together around me, indistinguishable from one another, I still vaguely understood what was happening. Memories and impressions flitted through my head—being hit, falling, an ambulance, the hospital, and pain. Lots of pain. And now I felt like I was swimming to the surface, or at least trying.

An antiseptic smell assaulted my nose, and the cuff squeezing my arm added to my discomfort. I could only hope I wasn't lying in a hospital gown for all the gals to see.

"I knew I shouldn't have let her leave the bakery." Lulu's voice carried the weight of guilt and concern. "I just don't know what I would've done if I'd lost her."

"You can't think like that." Polly's matter-of-fact tone cut through. "The doctor said she'll recover just fine. Our job is to help her get better."

Someone sniffled. I assumed it was Naomi.

"Why would she have been by herself in that parking lot?" Verity asked over the beeping of a machine. "She should have at least been paying attention to her surroundings. We've talked about that during our self-defense sessions."

Had I not been mulling over my encounter with Hamson, I would have been. And now I was paying the price with my head throbbing in time to the blood rushing in my ears. At least I was conscious.

"Do you think we ought to tell the police about the threat?" Naomi whispered.

"No." Polly's sharp voice jolted me to another level of wakefulness, though I had yet to pry open my eyes. "Don't you realize that if we tell them now, KC will be in trouble?"

"But this has gone too far," Lulu countered. "Maybe the cops can find some kind of a clue on the knife or the note that we missed."

"I hate to say it, but I'm with Polly on this," Verity said. "We'll all be in a good deal of trouble for not calling them last night when it happened. Unfortunately, I think we have to live with the choice we made, even if it was the wrong one."

"What if the person who did this to KC goes after her again… or comes for the rest of us, just like the note said?" Naomi's soft voice shook.

"That's why we have to stick together." Verity was adamant. "Think about it, though—we must be getting close to an answer. Otherwise, whoever hurt KC wouldn't have gone this far."

"Who knows what else they're capable of?" Lulu asked.

Verity sighed, and for a moment, there was silence. "You make a good point. I'm a little nervous going to David's house without her tonight." Her comment made no sense to me. Of course, I'd still go with her. As soon as I could wake myself up all the way. Did she think I'd let a little bonk on the head stop me?

"Verity, you will do no such thing. Going to David's is not happening." Lulu's tone was firm, and the others agreed.

How would we ever get to find out who Ruby was cutting out of her will if Verity and I missed our chance at David's? Surely he knew, and that could hold the key to the murder. I licked my lips, preparing to speak. With just a little more effort…

"Lulu's right. We don't want you to end up like KC." There were tears in Naomi's voice.

"Yeah, just look at her face," Polly said. "It's *mangled*."

I grunted, and finally, words came out of my mouth. "Hey, I can hear you." I peeled one eye open, then the other. Slowly, the curtained-off area came into focus.

My friends hovered over me—Polly and Naomi on the left and Lulu and Verity on the right. The worry on their faces made me wish I'd followed the code we'd come up with last night about sticking together. These were my people, and if any one of them were laying in this bed instead of me because they weren't careful, I'd have a conniption.

All at once, they spoke, bombarding me with questions I couldn't answer. What started out as hurried whispers rose to regular voices, then the usual clamor that followed the gang. My head pounded faster than their words.

"Who did this?"

"Did you get a good look?"

"Does it hurt, dear?"

"I'm going to rip their eyeballs out."

I opened my mouth to get a word in, but a raven-haired lady in a white coat parted the curtain that surrounded my bed. Her hands indicated everyone should settle down. "I'm sure you're all concerned about KC, but what she needs most right now are peace and quiet."

Naomi shook her head. "We're not very good at that." The others agreed.

"Can you tell us more about her prognosis?" Lulu asked.

While the doctor explained I would be fine, they'd given me drugs to curb the pain, and they needed to keep an eye on me, Naomi patted my arm and made cooing noises. Oddly, it soothed me. I should have paid attention to the doctor, but my mind trailed off in a hundred directions, mostly trying to figure out who did this to me and how I never saw it coming.

Clearly, what happened in the parking lot was connected to the threatening note last night. That meant that the killer believed we were zeroing in on them, even though none of us had strung the clues together enough to know. It also meant that the killer was following me—it was highly unlikely they were in the gym's parking lot so early in the morning by coincidence.

But who was it? David, Ella, Melody, Rick? It couldn't have been Walter. Whoever it was had come up behind me too quickly. I sighed with relief at the realization that our friend was more than likely in the clear, then I squeezed Naomi's hand. She offered me a knowing smile in return.

The curtain parted again, interrupting the doctor's spiel about rest and hydration.

Officer Leon offered a curt nod as she entered the small space, followed by Officer Kirby. "Sorry to interrupt, but it's important we speak to KC—now."

<hr>

THE CURTAINED-OFF area seemed to shrink the moment I was alone with the officers.

I glanced down to make sure I was clothed in more than a hospital gown. Thankfully, I still wore my workout clothes, though my leggings had a large scuff on the left knee, which throbbed the moment I noticed it.

Every part of my body ached more without my friends here to comfort me. My face, especially.

Officer Leon leaned closer to examine me, momentarily dropping her professional demeanor. Her sad smile contrasted with her smooth, dark skin. "That's going to hurt for a while."

How bad was my face, exactly? I felt more than a little self-conscious with the officer who should have been a supermodel scrutinizing me. I reached up to touch my cheek, dragging along a cord that was attached to my finger.

Just as quickly as she'd softened, Officer Leon turned stoic. "What can you tell us about the incident?"

It took me a moment to find my voice. "Who found me?"

Officer Kirby cleared his throat and glanced at his partner. "Another person who was there to work out. Tell us what happened."

"I came out of the gym." After an engaging conversation with Hamson. Speaking of… "Where is Officer Hamson?"

Officers Leon and Kirby exchanged a look. He spoke first. "Let's focus on you. We need to know what you remember."

I swallowed down the sadness rising in my chest over the fact these two were here instead of Hamson. Didn't he care at all what happened to me? The vibes he gave off showed that I was more to him than a passing acquaintance, and yet…he wasn't here. I was sick of his indecisive behavior—I deserved better. And I had half a mind to tell him so, but then he'd know I cared, and I definitely didn't want to go there. Maybe it only bothered me because my head hurt, and I was groggy. Yeah, that was it.

"KC?" Officer Leon prodded.

"What? Sorry." I shook myself out of my stupor. "When I came out of the gym, I guess I wasn't paying attention." Because of stupid Hamson. "And the sun, I think it was in my eyes. Or wait…I was looking in my gym bag for my keys. Usually, my car opens without me clicking it, but sometimes it doesn't."

Neither officer took notes, but both watched me intently.

I scraped my fuzzy memory for details. "I heard footsteps behind me."

"Where were you when you heard footsteps?" Officer Kirby asked.

"Coming up to the driver's side."

Officer Leon tilted her head. "Did you look back?"

I shook my head. "It happened too fast."

Kirby sighed. "So, you didn't get a good look at the perp?"

"No. I didn't see the person at all."

Officer Leon cleared her throat. "Any other indicators that you may have picked up on? Smells, sounds?"

The memory scared me as I recalled the moments before I blacked out. "I don't think so, other than the footsteps were quick."

"Was anything stolen?" Kirby asked.

I sat up a little, and the beeping sound from the monitor increased accordingly. "Where's my gym bag?"

The officers glanced around, then finally, Officer Leon pulled my bag out from somewhere behind my bed. "Is this it?"

"Yes, can I see it?" The moment she set it in my lap, I pawed through my belongings and pulled out my phone. "It looks like everything is here."

"So, robbery wasn't the motive." Officer Kirby quirked his eyebrows. "Why do you think someone did this to you?"

If I answered honestly, I'd be in trouble, both for interfering in the investigation of Ruby's murder and for not reporting last night's threat. But if I lied, they might never find who'd hurt me. I issued a non-committal grunt, then led with a question of my own. "Does the gym have cameras in their parking lot?"

Officer Leon spoke first. "We're headed there next." Her tone indicated there was more to the story, but she wasn't about to tell me.

"I wish I could remember what happened." I leaned back in the bed and took a deep breath, willing the beeping to slow down, along with my heart rate.

"I guess that about wraps it up, then." Officer Kirby gave a curt nod.

"Remember," Officer Leon said, "anything you tell us could be important. Here's my contact information." She pulled a card from her pocket and handed it to me. "*I'm* the one you need to stay in touch with regarding this case." It was as though she knew

I'd be inclined to call Hamson, but she was wrong. If he didn't care enough to take on my case himself, I had no more use for him, though the pang in my heart said otherwise.

It had to be the drugs. I wasn't *that* wrapped up in what Hamson did or didn't think of me.

Finally, the officers left, and I let out a long, slow breath, relieved they were gone. I turned on my phone, noting it was already approaching noon. Apparently, I'd been here a while. Against my better judgment, I thumbed open the camera app and turned it to selfie mode so I could see my face.

My poor, broken face.

Gingerly, I touched the goose egg on my forehead. Hadn't I been whacked from behind? I must've hit something on my way to meet the pavement, maybe the side-view mirror of my car. My nose was swollen and bruised, and my left cheek sported a gauze bandage. I hated to think about what was underneath.

The curtain parted again, and the doctor strode in. "Don't worry—it looks worse than it is."

I nodded, not quite believing her.

"I'm Doctor Kapoor." She extended her hand. "I don't think I properly introduced myself when your friends were here."

"I'm surprised you let them all in, to begin with." I attempted to chuckle, but even that hurt.

"Believe me, they can be persuasive."

"Tell me about it." I touched the lump on my head again. "Any lasting damage?"

Dr. Kapoor smiled. "You have a concussion, but you will fully recover."

"Oh, good." I started to sit up, noting the monitor beeping faster. "I'll just get going then."

"I don't think so." Dr. Kapoor frowned at me. "We'll be moving you out of the emergency department now that we've had a room open up. We'll be admitting you for further observation, just as a precaution. Someone will be in shortly to transport you." Her face opened with a bright, reassuring smile as she left.

Transport? Admit me?

It was noon now, and if they admitted me, I could be here a lot later than six o'clock when David's little soiree was scheduled to start. I did a few calculations as quickly as my sluggish mind would let me. How long before Verity canceled with David and made other plans? I should at least call her and tell her I was still game for going with her to the mansion.

I took another look at my face on the phone and winced. Maybe the doctor was right, and I needed to stay here.

Just then, a text popped onto my screen.

James.

Just checking in. Really starting to worry about you. Let me know you're ok.

Was I? At least he was asking, which was more than Hamson was doing. Not that James knew what happened this morning, but since I hadn't answered any of his messages, he was concerned. That was something.

I sighed, remembering the good times. My thumb hovered over the phone. If I answered, then he could quit worrying, and we could both move on. Texting him back was no big deal.

A bumpy day but I'm on the mend. Just trying to figure out if I'll be able to do what I need to do next.

I clicked send, then wished I could retract it. What a dumb thing to say, especially since it wouldn't make any sense to him.

On the mend? You sure you're ok? Anyway, you'll figure things out. Glad to hear from you.

Ugh, a cringey exchange, if ever there was one.

But James was right. I *would* figure things out.

With that, I peeled off the blood pressure cuff and the clip on my finger then grabbed my gym bag and scooted off the edge of the bed. I tested my unsteady legs, then said a quick prayer for strength. Slowly, I peeled back the curtain and looked left, then right. Dr. Kapoor ducked into another patient's area, and the nurses huddled at the desk.

Then, despite the pain coursing inside my head, I sucked in a fortifying breath and tiptoed toward the double doors that led to freedom.

Chapter Twenty-Two

THE FIRST THING I realized after making my escape from the
hospital was that I had no shoes.

Big mistake.

The second thing was that I also had no transportation.
Perhaps my concussion was a little worse than I thought. Clearly, I
hadn't planned my escape very well.

Pebbles stuck to the bottom of my feet as I picked my way
down the sidewalk, careful to avoid any hospital personnel who
may already have realized I was missing. As unlikely as it was, I
didn't want to take any chances that would compromise my
mission. I spotted a bench in a secluded area in the hospital's
courtyard under a large tree and hustled over to have a seat.

Quickly, I pulled up a ride-sharing app on my phone, but zero
cars dotted the screen, indicating I was out of luck. The gym was
only a mile or so from the hospital, but my feet were already
protesting. I'd have to find another way to get back to my car
unless I skipped picking it up and went to find Verity first.

Next, I opened the maps app, grateful my friend had set us up
for location sharing. A giant V sat at the corner of Pine and Third
—the library. She must've gone straight to work after visiting the
hospital. That was a lot closer than the gym. I could totally make

it a block and a half, despite the chill of the pavement and the pounding in my head.

"You can do this," I said, ignoring the stares of the couple walking past. "It's only half a mile." I girded myself for the cold and the pain, slid on my oversized sunglasses and left the security of the bench.

I tiptoed down the sidewalk and scurried across the street without waiting for the pedestrian indicator to change. Was I crazy, or was everyone watching me? If anyone reported back to Lulu and the gang that I was on the lam, I was toast. The hardest part of the whole day would be avoiding them until *after* David's party. Since we were all bunking together, I couldn't even go home to change. Hopefully, someone had remembered to feed Pooh Bear and take him for a walk, though I doubted he'd let anyone forget.

An abrupt honk pulled me from my musings. I hurried the rest of the way across the road, despite the pinpricks of the asphalt under my feet. Finally, the library was in sight. I stuck close to the buildings and kept my head down. Not that it would do much good with my zebra-striped hair. Anyone paying attention could tell it was me.

I hurried up the front steps, waited for an elderly man to pass through the door, then followed him inside. Verity stood at the reference desk, nodding solemnly at the person in front of her before tapping on her keyboard. I slid in line behind the patron—who seemed content to tell my friend every detail about the weather affecting their joints—and waved frantically.

Verity glanced up with shock in her eyes. I stopped waving. Perhaps that was over the top. She motioned for me to step to the side, so I sidled up next to a shelf full of audiobooks where I wouldn't be noticed.

Moments later, she rounded the desk and cuffed me by the elbow, dragging me into an empty study room. "What are you doing here?" She pointed to my feet. "And without shoes, too. That's against library policy."

"I may have left the hospital early—I mean, in a hurry."

Verity's mouth opened like a fish on a line. "Wait…you mean you weren't properly discharged?"

I scrunched my face at her. "You heard what the doctor said a half hour ago—they wanted to keep me for observation." Unless Verity hadn't, in fact, heard that part. The details were fuzzy, as was everything else in my head. Maybe I *wasn't* entirely well, but I didn't have time to think about that now.

She grabbed me by the shoulders. "You are going right back where you came from. There's no way you should be out of the hospital yet. It's called leaving against medical advice. That's serious stuff."

I stood firm. "I'm fine. Besides, if I'd stayed, I wouldn't be out in time to go to David's house tonight with you. Remember?" I prodded. "Our plan?"

"All of those plans went out the window when someone whacked you on the head. Speaking of which—" She glanced over me with a puzzled expression. "How did you get here?"

I bit my lip, in part to distract myself from the pain radiating from my skull. "I walked."

"That's the second time today you were by *yourself*—"

"It's fine." I grasped her flailing hands. "Trust me. It's all good." Never mind that she made a good point. Why hadn't I considered that whoever hurt me at the gym could have been waiting outside the hospital? Man, I needed to think things through.

"You need to get right back to the hospital, or your aunt will throttle me."

"No. I won't go, and you can't make me." I folded my arms like a petulant child. "If I go back, they won't let me out again until it's too late for the party. Don't you want to find out who did this to me?" I motioned to my injuries.

Verity's face softened, and her eyes flickered with uncertainty. "Of course I do."

"Then we have to go to David's house," I reasoned. "Whoever

did this to me is the same person who killed Ruby. I'm sure he has information that he doesn't even realize could be useful."

"I want you to get better, and ditching the hospital isn't helping."

I waved off her concern. "All they were going to do was stick me in a room and pop in every once in a while with a painkiller." *Which I could desperately use right now.* "I'll make you a deal—I'll hang out with you all day, and you can keep an eye on me. If I get worse instead of better, you can take me back." *Over my dead body.*

Verity pointed to my feet again. "You didn't even grab shoes."

"Minor detail."

"Fine." She dragged the word into at least three syllables. "It's not like I can make you do anything you don't want to, anyway."

I smiled smugly, and even that hurt. "I'll lie low in here," I said, goggling at the people who stared through the window of the study room as though I were a spectacle. "You can keep working while I figure out how we're going to use Bluetooth to communicate while you're inside David's house."

Verity flashed a quizzical look. "Duh—I'll use wireless earphones and have my phone in my pocket."

Oh. I should have thought of that.

"Are you sure you're okay?" Her voice slid up an octave.

I was as okay as one could be after getting whacked on the head then escaping the hospital barefoot. The bigger question was, would we find the Ice Cream Killer before they struck again?

For the rest of the afternoon, I waited in the study room.

Staying hidden after fleeing the hospital is harder than one would think. First, you have a billion doctors and nurses calling your cell phone and asking where you are and if you're okay. Second, life without pain killers is brutal, although, on the plus side, my brain sharpened after a few hours without meds. And third, hiding in a study room at the public library can be boring. Really boring.

Without my tablet to get some work done before the grand reopening tomorrow, I was left with my phone and a loaner laptop from the reference desk. It was enough for me to work out a spreadsheet with all the clues and the non-alibis of the key players.

It brought me back around to the fact that whoever murdered Ruby was most likely the phantom friend that she was supposed to meet at the ice cream shop—a person who'd never actually showed up, as far as anyone knew.

After tiring myself with clues, I made the rounds on my new clients' social media pages, adding my thumbs-up as the hundredth person on Jacob's latest post and the fourth on Trudi's. Those poor animals would never find a home if I didn't intervene. But there was only so much one could do with a giant knot on the back of their head and with their face—as Polly said—mangled.

Against my better judgment, I opened the camera app and examined my wounds. Grim. Perhaps I should have stayed in the hospital, but what would that accomplish? I was, however, a little surprised that the rest of the gang hadn't figured out that I was missing. Maybe they were too busy picking up my slack with the grand reopening preparations.

Verity burst into the study room. "Hurry, let's go."

"What?" Slowly, I rose, not realizing how unsteady my legs were after staying sedentary.

"The gang is on the move. I'm not sure if they're on their way to the hospital or not, but I know they're out of your house. We can swing by your place and grab shoes, then go to my place so I can change." Verity's eyes gleamed. "Then we can head to David's. We have a killer to catch."

Chapter Twenty-Three

WHEN VERITY STEPPED out of her bedroom, I gasped. Within ten minutes, she'd changed herself entirely. Her plaid flannel was replaced by a little black off-the-shoulder dress, and with her red hair in a glamorous updo, she looked positively regal.

"Don't look so surprised." She narrowed her eyes, clearly having read my mind.

I smiled, despite the throbbing pain in my head. "You're actually glowing."

"Well, I wouldn't go that far." Verity blushed.

Secretly, I hoped David wasn't guilty of Ruby's murder, for Verity's sake. It seemed she actually liked him—at least enough to care about her appearance tonight.

She shook her head. "Oh no you don't. This isn't about me trying to impress anyone. This is me, going undercover."

"In that case, you need to take your hair down."

"Why? I think it looks good this way." She touched the back.

"It does, for sure. But," I said, pulling out the sparkly clip, "your wireless earbuds will show." I grinned and pointed to my temple. "See, I told you I'm feeling better. I'm back in top form." Except for my aching face.

We headed for my place, where Pooh Bear offered an enthusiastic greeting. By the time I changed, grabbed some snacks for Pooh for the short ride, and left again, I was more than a little sad that no one had noticed I was missing from the hospital yet. But that sadness was short-lived when I received a frantic call from Aunt Lulu, with Polly screeching in the background.

Bleep, bleep, bleep.

At the sound of expletives, I pulled the phone away from my ear and put it on speaker. Then I glanced at Verity, who was driving. "I'm almost sorry I picked up." Pooh Bear woofed from the front seat, agreeing with me.

"You know good and well you should be in the hospital right now." Clearly, my aunt was attempting to moderate her tone... and failing miserably. "I insist you come back right now and check yourself back in."

I glanced down at my cute blue and white printed dress and heeled slingbacks. Though I hadn't been invited to this evening's soiree, as the others had pointed out, there was no reason for me not to look the part. "It's a bit late now. We're already on our way. In fact," I said as David's mansion loomed at the edge of the bluff, "we're almost there."

More expletives sounded in the background. The pounding in my head intensified.

"What Polly is trying to say," said Lulu, "is that we can't understand why you'd be on your way to the house of someone who is still *under suspicion*." The way she punctuated her words caused me to picture her with her teeth bared, lips trembling.

"Well, I'd like to figure out who—as Polly said—*mangled my face*." It hurt to even say the words. "Also, we still need to find Ruby's killer."

"Not if you're putting yourselves at great risk." Lulu's terse words caused me to shrivel inside, just like when she caught me sneaking home late as a teen.

"That's right! You tell her." Naomi chimed in.

"We're not at risk. We're together." I smiled at Verity, who looked at me in the rearview mirror. "Remember, she's an expert in self-defense. David should be afraid of *her*."

Verity scowled at me.

"Not that he's the one who did it." I quickly backpedaled. "In any case, the key to Ruby's death may be in his house. I think we need to take a look at that appointment book. That probably has the person who she was supposed to meet penciled in." I tried to sound more confident than I felt. "I'm not giving up."

"But you don't know what you two are walking in—"

I grabbed a discarded potato chip bag off the floor and started crinkling it into the speaker. "I think we're breaking up."

"That's a chip bag," Naomi said in the background. "She tried that as a kid, remember?" Murmurs of agreement sounded over the line.

"*Fine.* I've got to go. We'll call you when we're finished." I disconnected and let out a whoosh of air.

Verity tsked me. "Have you no shame?"

I suppressed an eye roll. "Look, I'm a little new to this telling-the-truth-at-all-costs thing. Besides, they saw right through me."

She scoffed. "It's not that hard, is it Pooh-Pooh Bear?" She scratched his ears, earning his approval.

Traitor.

Moments later, we pulled through the open gate and drove down the expansive drive until it circled the front of the cavernous house. I slid lower in the backseat to avoid being seen. The sky was edging towards darkness, the sun sinking low on the Pacific. No other cars were in sight, and all of a sudden, David's cover story about a get-together sounded a little too flimsy.

Apprehension swirled in my gut. Even Pooh Bear stuck his head out the window and took a sniff, then emitted a low growl. "I don't like the looks of this. Are you sure his text said six o'clock? It's already twenty after, and no one else is here." While that would have been the norm for a gathering in LA., in Beaver Bluff, it was plain bad manners.

"I'm sure everyone else will be here soon." Verity's unsure

tone didn't match her words. She maneuvered the car around the circular driveway until it pointed back the way we came. At least that would make for a quicker getaway, should it become necessary. She put the car in park, then checked herself out in the rearview mirror, smacking her lips when she was finished.

I raised my head over the seat just a fraction and peered toward the manor. "Are you sure this is a good idea?"

"Would you quit being a baby?" She placed a wireless earbud in her left ear. "You're full of bravado when it's *you* taking chances, but when it comes to me, you're starting to sound like the rest of the gang."

In my defense, it felt different when it was someone else's butt on the line. I sat a little higher. "If I were going inside with you, it would be different. Instead, I'll be out here and can't do anything to help."

"You said it yourself. *I'm* the self-defense expert, so chill out." She opened the car door but paused to look back at me, then she motioned to my phone. "You'll hear if anything starts to go wrong. Now, dial me up, and let's get this party started."

<hr>

I SWITCHED TO WIRELESS EARBUDS, then stuffed my phone into the front of my dress, like Naomi, before sliding out of the car. The door clicked softly when I closed it, but the sound echoed off the outside walls of the house. I paused before proceeding.

Pooh Bear stuck his snout out the window and whined.

"Not now." I shushed him.

"Stop talking," Verity said in my ear.

Oops. This was going to take some getting used to. "Sorry." I waved to her as she approached the front door.

She reached up to ring the bell without giving me a chance to hide in the shadows.

Quickly, I scuttled off the gravel and into the grass on the side of the driveway, crouching low. I hurried to get to the flowery shrubs up ahead before David answered the door. At the bushes, I tiptoed closer to the house, grateful that I'd regained my balance and my wits after this morning's trauma. "Remember, do whatever you have to do to get David out of the room. Then try to find that appointment book."

"Duh," she whispered just as the massive door swung open.

I peeked through the bushes to get a better look. A cool breeze blew in off the ocean, and I hoped the crashing waves wouldn't keep me from hearing what was happening inside the house.

"Hey there." David appeared, wearing a black turtleneck and jeans that looked a little too snug. Even in the scant light, his eyes gleamed, and he flashed a wolfish grin. "So glad you could make it. Come on inside." Hearing his voice both in person and in my earbud made me dizzy. I was half-glad they went inside, but at the same time, alarm bells rang in my chest. I drew a deep, calming breath.

"Wow, you've done some really…interesting…things to the place," Verity said.

"Do you like it?" David's voice echoed in the entryway. "Gran never let me make any of the decorating decisions. I thought a few minor changes would liven things up."

"Uh…yeah…I think the safari motif is…unique." Verity's voice quivered.

I tittered in response. "I can't wait to hear the rest of your compliments. Be totally *honest*," I admonished.

"Shut…" Verity paused abruptly. "*Off*…yes, I shut *off* the car." Verity offered a soft growl.

"Are you worried about your car?" David asked, his voice smooth and polite. "I'll walk you outside, and we can check."

"No, no. I'm sure it's fine. So…where is everyone else?"

David blew off her question. "Let's retire to the library for drinks."

Yes, the library—that's where we last saw Ruby's appointment book! I crept along the outside wall toward the corner window, fairly certain that was the same room they'd be in, though it was hard to remember the floor plan after having only visited once.

"How have you been, David? I've been concerned about you."

"You know how it goes. Grief can hit you at the strangest times. It's been a hard week." His voice cracked.

I strained to hear his words over the fallen leaves crunching underfoot as I continued along the wall. The ground sloped, creating a wider separation between my line of sight and the bottom ledge of the window, where a sliver of light shone through. If I could just see inside, I could offer some help.

"Have you heard anything more from the police?" Verity kicked into investigative mode.

"Unfortunately, no. They're keeping me in the dark."

The window ledge protruded about a foot above my head. I glanced around for something to stand on. A rock rested close enough to the foundation for me to scoot it the rest of the way, but I still wasn't tall enough for me to see inside.

I stood on the rock and reached up, clasping my fingers onto the ledge. Slowly, I pulled myself higher, the same way Griff made me do a million times on the chin-up bar at the gym. My toes skidded against the side of the house but finally found purchase. I finagled my way higher until I could see beneath the window shade into the library.

David and Verity entered the room, and he spoke first. "I've just been trying to keep myself busy, trying new things. It keeps my mind off...well, you know."

My gaze swept the room, landing on the desk close to the window facing the ocean. But where was the planner? As far as I could see, it was not open on the desk as it had been when we were here before. "See if you can get him out of the room," I whispered.

Just then, an enormous dog with long gray and white fur bounded into the room, startling Verity from behind. "Oh, my. Who is this big guy?" Her green eyes widened as the dog gave her the sniff test.

"This is Bruno." David reached down and ruffled the dog's fur. "He's really friendly unless he doesn't know you, of course."

Verity tried to back away, but Bruno followed. "Uh…help?"

"Bruno, come." David reached out and tugged at his collar. "I got him to help keep me company now that Gran is gone." He released an Oscar-worthy sigh. "I'll put him out now. Be right back." He and Bruno left the library.

"Hurry," I said. "Go to the desk and see if you can find the appointment book. I don't think it's on top, so you'll have to look through the drawers."

Verity scurried to the desk. "That seems like an awful breach of privacy."

"If you don't do it, I'll come knock on the door and do it myself."

"As if." Her eyes scanned the different windows. "Where are you, anyway?"

"At the front window." I gave a little knock, which caused me to almost lose my grip.

Her eyes slivered in my direction until she found me, then she nodded. "Just keep out of sight."

"Don't worry about me. Just find the book."

A door slammed at the ocean-side of the house. Bruno woofed.

I froze. "Is there any chance the dog is inside a fenced yard?"

Verity looked out the window near the desk. "Nope. He's coming your way."

Bruno barked again, this time louder. Pooh Bear answered from the car. Giant dog steps sounded around the corner. He was coming my way.

Quickly, I slid down the wall and scurried away from the house. If I could just get to the car before Bruno found me, I'd be okay, and I would still be able to hear what was happening, even though I wouldn't be able to see.

Small rocks and leaves popped under my shoes. I moved faster, my heart jack-hammering inside my chest. My breath came in short spurts as I tried to keep quiet.

Bruno barked, signaling he'd marked me as a target.

I ran faster, unconcerned about the noise.

Pooh Bear barked harder, daring Bruno to keep chasing me. The car rocked as Pooh tried to find a way out.

"What's going on?" David's voice sounded in my ear.

"Uh…nothing much?" Verity answered.

I glanced over my shoulder, noting how fast Bruno lumbered towards me, despite his big, puffy body.

"Something's happening outside. I'd better check," David said.

The car was twenty yards ahead. My lungs labored for breath, and my ankles throbbed as they twisted and turned over the uneven ground.

Running in heels could kill a girl.

Time moved in slow motion as I neared the car, breathless. Pooh Bear's barks did nothing to fend off Bruno, who moved ever closer. I could feel him behind me. In mere moments, I'd be shredded to bits. Then this would all be for nothing, and I'd never know who killed Ruby and attacked me. Bruno nipped at my backside, tugging my dress.

All of a sudden, a shout rent the air. "Bruno, stop!"

The dog halted just as I reached the car and turned to see David standing at the front door, his features darkened with anger. "I demand to know what's going on!"

Chapter Twenty-Four

"HEE-YA!" Verity's shout and fighting stance caused David to fall back without her even having to touch him. Also, she split my eardrums.

David held his hands up in a surrender position, his backside pinned to the front door. "Verity, what's gotten into you? What's going on?" He spoke with a strange combination of fear and wonder in his voice, probably at Verity's sudden transformation.

"You can't yell at my friend." Slowly she straightened and dropped her hands to her sides.

David brushed the front of his shirt, then pulled it taut. "I didn't know that the person running from my house was your friend." He squinted to get a better look. "Oh, it's *you*. I thought I told you to stay away from me."

I rubbed Pooh Bear's ears to calm his barking, then opened the door for him to hop out. Pooh and Bruno gave each other the sniff test while I headed toward David and Verity, where I joined them on the veranda. The dogs trotted off and started happily circling the driveway.

David folded his arms defiantly but then eased up when I got close. "What happened to your face?"

"Why don't *you* tell me?" I challenged as I pulled out the earbuds.

"If I knew, I wouldn't be asking." He resumed his defensive stance. "It doesn't matter. The point is, why are you at my house?"

Why, indeed? Going with the truth sounded like a bad idea. I stalled. "Well…I heard there was a get-together tonight."

He shook his head. "You weren't invited."

Why did everyone have to keep reminding me?

I fisted my hands on my hips, trying to look stronger than I felt. "That's beside the point. Where is everyone else?" I swept my hand around the circular drive that was empty except for Verity's car. "Why, exactly, were you trying to lure my friend here? It's a good thing I came with her." Never mind that she could clearly take care of herself.

Verity's eyes narrowed as she turned to David. "Yeah, why *did* you invite me to your so-called get-together?"

David raked his hand through his dark hair, then poised his finger to his mouth. Finally, he shook his head and issued a defeated sigh. "Both of you come inside." His jaw ticked. "I have a confession to make, and I'm not about to do it out here."

* * *

VERITY'S earlier remark about David's new décor didn't do the safari motif justice.

Gone were the garish vases and art that flaunted money. Instead, a giraffe-print wall hanging adorned the foyer, and I was almost certain I could hear a jungle-themed soundtrack playing softly through the hidden speakers.

Despite the fact I was desperate to hear David's confession, I second-guessed our decision to follow him into the mansion, especially without Pooh Bear, who insisted on playing outside with his new pal Bruno. But now that David was ready to confess, he seemed more resigned than angry. Not to mention the odds of overpowering Verity and me both were a lot slimmer than taking out an elderly woman with a cane.

"Right this way." David led us over a leopard-print rug toward the library, guarded by giant lion statues on either side of the door. "As I was telling Verity, I've made a few changes since Gran's passing. She never let me have a say while she was alive."

With good reason.

Verity and I followed David into the library with the large windows overlooking the ocean. When he wasn't looking, I pulled my phone from the front of my dress and opened an app to record our conversation. Even if it wasn't admissible in court, it would point the authorities in the right direction.

"You certainly have your own sense of style, *David Maxwell*." I enunciated clearly for the recording.

He flashed a quizzical look but proceeded to talk. "Yes, I may have gone a little wild with my new freedoms over the last few days."

"Yes, I heard that you and your grandma were not getting along." I studied his face for telltale signs.

He shrugged. "Everyone has their issues. In any case, I am enjoying my new freedom. I decorated, I brought Bruno home." His mouth quirked as though he were quite pleased with himself. "I even joined a rock-climbing club."

That explained the rope!

I tried not to look surprised. "Sounds like you have a whole new life with your grandmother out of the way."

He gasped. "Out of the way? That's an awful thing to say. It's more like I've been looking for ways to stay distracted. Please," David said, his hand sweeping toward the sofa in the center of the stately room, "have a seat."

I fisted my hands. "Not without you telling us why you lured Verity here under the pretense of a party."

David's forehead wrinkled, and he shook his head slightly. "Lured is such a strong word."

"And what about the confession you wanted to make?" Verity

stood beside me, and though she appeared relaxed, I could tell from our weeks of practice that she was ready to roundhouse our so-called host before he knew what hit him.

"If I'm going to confess, I'd at least like to do it sitting, if you don't mind." He situated himself on the loveseat, his eyes fixed on Verity. "I'm a little nervous."

We glanced at each other, then at David. Slowly, we lowered ourselves onto the sofa, but without making ourselves comfortable.

"There's nothing to be nervous about. Just tell us in your own words what happened." Verity spoke with a soothing tone.

"What do you mean, 'what happened?'" David sat straighter. "The only thing that happened was I invited Verity to arrive before the others."

Verity and I shared a look.

"Why?" I asked.

A red hue crept into David's clean-shaven face. He gazed at the zebra-striped decorative pillow next to him before looking at Verity. "It's simple—I wanted a few minutes alone with her."

"But *why*?" I prodded.

Verity slapped my thigh. "Don't you get it? He likes me." She spoke between clenched teeth.

"What?" My gaze volleyed between the two of them…who were making eyes at each other. "Oh, good grief." I massaged my aching temple. "And what about your confession?"

David's head snapped toward me. "That *was* the confession. What did you think it was?"

I rolled my eyes. "Oh, I don't know. Maybe something about your grandmother and the ongoing case?"

"Didn't I already tell you? The police are keeping me in the dark." He offered a sad shrug.

I held my phone to my mouth. "Never mind. I think we hit a dead end."

David gasped, then pointed at Verity and me. "Wait…what do you mean? What were you trying to do?"

"Apparently, nothing." I rubbed the side of my head as I tried to think of a new line of questioning.

"Hold on." David held his hands in front of him. "Were you here spying on me? I knew you were hinting around the other day at the salon when I saw you, but—"

"Well, you lied. You weren't getting your hair done when your grandmother was murdered."

David had the good sense to look sheepish. "You're right."

"So, where were you then?" Verity's sharp voice startled David and me both. He had *no* idea how much she hated lying.

"That day, I felt horrible once I found out what happened, and I was too embarrassed to admit that I'd left her side. If only I'd been there…." David's eyes moistened. "The truth is, I went in to make an appointment for my haircut, but I just didn't feel like going back and sitting with Gran and whoever she was meeting for ice cream. So I was just hanging out at the square, and that's when the gun went off."

"That was so scary." Verity placed her hand on her chest.

"Right?" David said. "I mean, he could have shot anyone, including his poor wife. Did you hear the way she berated him for showing off his gun?"

I perked. "You heard that?"

"We all did, didn't we?" He glanced between us. "I was a little farther away from the man than you two were, at least when those cops came and made us stand back."

Verity's face brightened. "You really were at the square—you couldn't have hurt your grandmother."

David's face wrinkled. "Of course not. What kind of man do you think I am?"

One with incredibly bad taste in home décor but incredibly fabulous taste in women.

I sank against the sofa and cuddled a zebra pillow to my chest. "You're not mad at us, are you? We just want to find out who killed your grandmother."

David flashed a hopeful smile. "I'm glad you care about what happened to her. She could be pretty blunt, but in her own way, she had a soft heart. I'll do anything to help you find out who did it."

I sat up. "Can we see her appointment book?"

David frowned. "Sure, but why?" Slowly, he rose and went to the desk by the ocean-view window. "Oh, look—some of the other guests are arriving now."

"Then we'll need to hurry." I quickly joined him at the desk, and Verity followed.

He removed her book from the top drawer and handed it over to Verity. "What do you think is in here?"

She slapped it onto the desk and started flipping through the pages.

I glanced out the side window. Thankfully, Pooh Bear and Bruno started harassing the other party-goers, keeping them from the front door. Still, it would only buy us a few minutes. "Hurry, before the others come inside."

David hovered over our shoulders, trying to get a look. "What is it? What do you see?"

"Your grandma's lawyer's secretary told us she was planning to meet with someone that she was writing out of her will." I kept my gaze fixed on the book rather than looking at David.

"That sounds like her. She usually did that to give them a chance to convince her otherwise. She always said that a lot of organizations needed her money, so she had to choose wisely." The nostalgia in David's voice tugged at my heart, if only a little.

"Don't you see?" Verity asked over her shoulder. "That could have been a motive for murder. And don't you think it's a little strange that whoever she was supposed to meet never showed up that day?"

The doorbell gonged.

"Wait, don't answer yet." I cuffed David's shoulder. "Please, give us a minute."

"Here it is." Verity stabbed her finger on the page and read aloud. "The only meeting she had that day was at Yum Yum's with someone named Ermantrude."

We both looked at David. He offered a slow shrug. "I guess that's one of her charity people. I don't actually know them all."

"Ermantrude," I repeated slowly. Thoughts formed in my head, images and clues snapping together like a jigsaw puzzle. "One of three people who always likes the animal shelter posts is named Erman. That has to be the same person."

This time, it was Verity and David who shared a look. They spoke at the same time. "And?"

The doorbell rang again.

"I can't believe I didn't see it before, but I know who did it." I covered my mouth.

David pointed at the book. "Someone named Erman killed my grandma?"

I nodded vigorously. "There's no time to explain. We've got a lot to do to make sure this person is caught." I grabbed Verity's arm and tugged her toward the foyer.

"I'll do whatever I can to help," David said as he trailed us.

"Good," I said, stopping abruptly. "I'm going to need you at the grand reopening tomorrow, and I'll also need you to write a fat check."

"YOUR FACE LOOKS WORSE than I thought." Concern lined Hamson's eyes.

I stood under the porch light in the doorway of his home, indignant but determined to fulfill my mission. "As if you care."

"Of course I care." His sincere tone was Oscar-worthy, but I wasn't falling for it.

"Sure, that's why you were at the hospital to check on me—oh wait, you weren't." I locked eyes with Hamson, but the gentleness of his gaze almost caused me to lose focus. After this morning's assault, escaping the hospital, and figuring out who the murderer was, I was exhausted and maybe a little vulnerable. Or a lot vulnerable.

"You came all the way to my house to see why I wasn't at the hospital?" The smooth undertones in his voice mesmerized me, and the way his gaze swept over my face only intensified the vulnerability. Why did I want him to care so badly? It wasn't like he and I could ever be a thing, especially not if I planned to eventually head back to the city.

I tore loose from his dark gaze. "Never mind all that. I came here because I need your help."

He glanced at the floor where his cat did a figure eight between us and meowed. "Sure."

"I know you think I'm crazy, and you don't want to get—"

"KC, I said yes." Hamson tucked an errant strand of hair behind my ear, his thumb hovering near my bruises. My face tingled at his touch.

The cat meowed again, causing Hamson and me to step apart.

"Hey there, big fella." I leaned down and picked up Figaro, the fat tuxedo cat. "Remember me?" I scratched behind his ears, and he rewarded me with a deep purr.

"What do you need help with?" Hamson casually leaned against the doorframe and joined me in petting Figaro.

"Tomorrow is the grand reopening of Crumbs."

He grinned. "You think your aunt or any of her friends would let me forget? I'll definitely be there. Do you want me to bring something?"

"Yeah—backup."

Hamson choked, then coughed. "Wait, hold up. Please don't tell me you're still in this after I warned you."

My mouth puckered. "I think we both knew that wasn't going to work."

"Are you trying to tell me you know who killed Ruby?"

I nodded. "Yes, and I've added a huge incentive to the giveaways tomorrow to make sure that person is there."

"Don't tell me you're going to go all Agatha Christie and get the suspects in a room together for the big reveal."

"Unless you have a better idea." Quickly, I recounted all the facts as I knew them, trying to focus on the case and not the casual way his hand brushed mine as we petted Figaro. "And that's when I knew who did it. It all makes sense."

Uncertainty flickered in Hamson's eyes as he weighed the evidence. "Why couldn't you just let the staties do their job?"

I pointed to my face.

Hamson fisted his hands on his waist, then pinched the bridge of his nose. "You realize I could lose my job over all this."

I searched his gaze. "Yes, but a woman lost her life."

Hamson's features softened under the porch light. "I don't know if you're even right about all this, and it's against my better judgment, but I'll be there."

Chapter Twenty-Five

AN AUTUMN STORM moved into Beaver Bluff the next morning. Thunderclouds hovered low over the town, and gusts of wind swept off the ocean, adding to the chill in the air. I could only pray the new incentive of a five-thousand-dollar donation to the winner's charity of choice would be enough to entice everyone to join us at Crumb's.

As soon as we'd left David's last night, I'd sent out an e-blast to everyone on my invite list, telling them about the added bonus for the grand prize winner. Even though a year of baked treats was, in my opinion, enough of a prize, I had to make sure the killer showed up no matter what—must be present to win.

By eleven o'clock, I realized I needn't have worried as people trickled in and purchased scones, muffins, breads, and other tasty treats. Krystal worked the counter while Verity and Polly helped with tables and cleanup. Naomi and I staffed the different stations for smaller drawings with gift cards and other prizes. Aunt Lulu and the ever-elusive Bert worked the kitchen, continually pumping out more goodies as the hour wore on.

"Look, it's almost noon." Naomi pointed to the cat clock with her dishtowel in a rare moment the gang and I had a chance to huddle up.

Verity's eyes scanned the swelling crowd. "I still don't see you-know-who."

I didn't either, and I was more than a little nervous the killer wouldn't even show. I took a large bite of cupcake to hide my nerves.

Griff's shoulder bumped me.

I hid my cupcake behind my back and smiled.

"Glad to see you're on the mend." He motioned to the side of his mouth to indicate I had something on mine.

I wiped the frosting. "Thanks. It was a scary day, that's for sure." I thanked him for coming, then he and Holly moved along. Which reminded me, I still needed to tell her about the front door.

"What's the plan, again?" Naomi asked as Lulu joined us.

Quickly, I corralled the gang in the kitchen, away from prying ears. "The idea is to get you-know-who to confess, in the kitchen, in front of Hand…I mean, Hamson."

Polly leaned in. "How are you even going to do that?"

"We'll do the grand prize drawing, where you-know-who is going to win." I glanced around to make sure Bert wasn't listening. "Then we'll bring them back here to finalize the details."

"Wait a sec." Verity stage whispered. "You mean the drawing is rigged?"

"Shh," the rest of us admonished.

"Of course not. We'll draw the real winner later." I pulled the gang closer. "Once they're back here in the kitchen, we'll confront them with the evidence while Hamson listens in from the break room."

"Does he know that's what he's supposed to do?" Naomi took a bite of her scone, smearing her coral-colored lipstick.

"Not exactly." I shook my head.

"This doesn't seem like something Hamson would agree to." Lulu wiped her hands on a dishtowel.

I looked each one of my friends in the eye. "Don't worry, this will work itself out. Trust me."

The gang groaned in unison. Polly spoke first. "But he *will* be here, right?" She waved her arms around, presumably to demonstrate his absence.

My stomach clamped. "Hamson said he would. I'm sure he'll keep his word." But somehow, I wasn't altogether certain. The idea that he'd change his mind wasn't far-fetched, especially considering he was concerned about his job, and helping us would hurt his image on the force.

Verity looked through the window on the swinging door. "We'd better get back out there. More people just showed up."

We shuffled back out to the dining area.

"Look who the cat dragged in." Naomi nudged me and pointed toward the door with her lips.

Ella breezed into Crumb's and was greeted by a few of our regulars, then she joined the end of the queue at the counter. It was all I could do to keep from grimacing at her. Instead, I drew a deep breath. "We'd better all get back to work. It's almost showtime."

The huddle split like pool balls on a table, each of us scurrying off to carry out our duties. I headed for the main stage set up against the sidewall and started preparing for the grand prize drawing. At some point in the rush, David walked in.

"Sorry I'm late. It was all I could do to get here." He glanced around surreptitiously. "I don't see—"

"Shh." Thankfully, the mic wasn't yet turned on. "We'll wait just a few more minutes."

The door opened, and another influx of people came in and within moments were in front of me, filling out entries for the grand prize.

My gaze volleyed around all the full tables. Ella was sitting with one of her waitstaff, and Melody occupied an adjacent table. Rick sat near a table of freebies, chatting up my hairstylist—I'd have to have a word with her later—while eyeballing his soon-to-be-ex-wife, presumably to make her jealous.

As people chatted and made their way from table to table, my heart filled with appreciation for my fellow Beaver Bluffians. Practically everyone I knew had shown up, even Walter, who was making eyes at Naomi. If only I could focus solely on today and what it meant for Crumb's Bakery, but instead, I needed to trap a killer.

"Don't worry—they'll be here." I grabbed David and quickly pulled him next to me for a selfie, as I'd already done with several others, regardless of my bruises. I had to keep up the facade, and besides, it helped keep me calm.

David and I continued to mingle with others throughout the bakery while I mentally ran through the plan. I'd announce the winner from the stage, then calmly take the perp into the kitchen, where Hamson would be listening in from the break room off to the side. I would ask them to fill out paperwork with their charity of choice, then casually ask them to put their legal name— Ermantrude—in the blank, thus confirming my suspicions.

Another wave of people rolled through the front door, including Antonio Hamson, wearing a dark flannel with gray khakis. Relief tunneled through me, knowing he was here. I motioned to Polly to usher him to the back. She caught him by the crook of his arm and marched him toward the kitchen.

Then I caught the perp in the corner of my eye. My pulse jumped. David elbowed me, then I elbowed Verity, and Naomi elbowed Polly as she returned from the kitchen. I took a deep breath. It was time to get the show started.

I quickstepped up to the stage and switched on the mic. "All right, everyone, welcome to the grand reopening of Crumb's Bakery."

Cheers erupted from the crowd. A few final people, including the killer, stuffed their entries into the ballot box, then retreated toward the counter. At this point, it was standing room only, but no one seemed to mind. Lulu stepped out from the kitchen, her face beaming with joy.

"And here's the mastermind behind the bakery, Lulu Crumb!" I swept my hand in her direction, and more applause and a few whistles added to the cacophony. "Thank you for coming out today. Crumb's Bakery has been here for almost twenty years, and we plan to be here for many more Crummy years!"

"Many years!" someone shouted.

David motioned me with his eyes toward the killer, who appeared restless. Then he mouthed, "Get on with it."

I waited for the applause to die. "Without further ado, we're going to do the grand drawing for a five-thousand-dollar donation to the charity of the winner's choice, courtesy of David Maxwell." I reached down, grabbed his arm, and pulled him onto the stage.

A red hue tinted his cheeks when I held the microphone to him. "Truly, it's my pleasure." His shoulders heaved with a deep breath. "As most of you know, my grandmother was recently killed."

A murmur ran through the crowd. I glanced at the murderer, who shifted, angling toward the front door.

"But I want to continue her legacy of charitable giving, so today's grand prize is in honor of my grandmother, Ruby Maxwell." David's voice cracked.

Polite applause sounded at each table, and for that, I was grateful. Even though she'd made a number of enemies over the years, she had been charitable. And no one deserved to be brutally punished the way she was for their character flaws.

David handed the mic back to me. I cuffed his shoulder in a show of support. "And without further ado, we're going to draw. The person must be present to win." I stuffed my hand into the box and stirred the entries, top to bottom and bottom to top. I then made a show of closing my eyes and sent up a quick prayer that no one would ask to see the form.

Suddenly, people started drum-rolling on the tables, causing my adrenaline to flow a little faster.

I pulled an entry out and opened the folded paper. My heart thudded in my chest. The actual winner and the killer were one and the same. "And the winner is…Trudi Bucket!" I turned my attention toward the counter, where she covered her mouth and gasped. Then she fanned herself with her hand. "Come on up, Trudi."

Her face turned bright red as she shook her head. "No, no. I'll call you, and we can square it away," she stammered. Then she tried to push her way to the front door. Apparently, David's mentioning Ruby had scared her.

"Meet me in the kitchen…I need your information," I pleaded with her.

"I'll be in touch," she called over her shoulder. If I didn't do something, she would get away.

"Wait!" The mic squealed when I shouted.

A hush fell over the crowd. Even Trudi paused, wide-eyed, caught between Jacob from the adventure camp and someone who appeared to be his lady friend.

"She did it," David shouted in a rush. "She killed my grandmother!"

Well, that didn't go according to plan. I turned to shush him while keeping my eye on Trudi.

She tried to ease past Jacob. "I don't know what you're talking about."

Everyone in the crowd turned to her, and her face changed from deep red to purple.

"Trudi, please come to the kitchen, and we can sort this out," I said calmly.

"If she's a killer, I think you should draw a new winner," someone heckled from the crowd.

"Don't worry, we will," I answered.

"This is ridiculous." Rage flashed in Trudi's eyes. "It could've been anyone. No one actually liked her."

David gasped.

Trudi rolled her eyes, seeming to gather strength while forgetting her usual quiet disposition.

"Believe me, there were a number of people I suspected." I handed the mic to David as I stepped off the stage as everyone watched. "I thought it could have been Rick or Melody—sorry guys." I flashed them a look. "Either one could have taken the back hallway into Walter's shop and killed Ruby when everyone was across the street after the gunshot. After all, she was murdered with a rope—the same kind Rick sells at his store. And Ruby did spread damaging gossip about them."

People muttered in agreement while both Rick and Melody grumbled in my direction.

"Or it could have been Ella." I shrugged at the bistro owner.

"Hey!" she snapped at me.

"Ruby drove you out of business. You, too, could have taken the back hallway and not been seen by anyone as you snuck in to strangle Ruby."

"What does this have to do with me?" Trudi's mouth tightened. "I don't have a back hallway, and Ruby didn't gossip about me. She was a big supporter of the animal rescue. Why would I want her dead?"

"Because while she may have supported the rescue currently, she *was* going to cut your charity out of her will. And I'll bet that's where the *big* money was. She was about to let you know that day at Walter's shop, but when the gun went off, and everyone was across the street, you took advantage of the moment."

The crowd gasped. I pressed forward, and people parted until there was no one standing between Trudi and me.

"How would you know? Besides, I'm sure she put people in and out of her will all the time. She could be fickle like that." Trudi glanced around as if looking for someone to take her side.

"When I heard from someone at Ruby's lawyer's office that she was taking someone out of her will, I actually suspected David, thinking he wanted to kill her before she could do it." I offered an apologetic look.

He shrugged. "I understand."

"I didn't catch on right away, but once I saw her appointment book for the day she died and saw your name, I put it together." I tapped the side of my head.

"My name was not in her appointment book." Trudi folded her arms.

"Well, it's true that the name Trudi was not in there." I paced between two tables, noting everyone's gazes following. "I remembered you mentioned that you only get traction on a social media post if someone likes it right away." I looked at the crowd. "It's true. Algorithms work that way sometimes. But I happened to notice that the same people always liked your animal rescue posts—Mary, Tom, and Erman. Then I thought back to the time that you asked what my name stands for, mentioning that your name was also short for something you didn't care for. Apparently, that name is *Ermantrude*."

Trudi's eyes widened, first with surprise, then with rage. She started to move toward the front door. Jacob blocked her, and as she tried another angle, Griff stepped in for the intercept. Then Trudi pivoted and bolted for the kitchen, shoving aside Naomi and Polly, who grasped each other to maintain balance.

Anger propelled me forward. She might have bludgeoned me on the head, but no one messed with my friends.

I hurried towards her, then tugged at her shirt. She jerked away, pushing past Holly and another woman. Then I cut in front of Trudi just before she reached the swinging door, and with a sweep of my leg, I pulled her feet from under her. "Hee-ya!"

Trudi's arms windmilled, and as if in slow motion, she fell forward, ending up...in Hamson's grip, as he saved her from crashing to the floor.

"What's your hurry?" Hamson steadied her, his neutral cop-like expression stopping her cold. "I think you have some explaining to do."

"What's wrong with you people?" Trudi tried to wiggle out of his grasp, to no avail. "Do you all hate animals or something?"

"Oh, brother," Polly said. "No, but we *do* have a thing against murderers."

David spoke into the mic. "Let's hear it for your favorite sleuth and mine—KC Crumb!"

One person started to clap, then another, then another, until finally, Crumb's Bakery was awash in cheers and hollers. The crowd chanted my name, fists pumping in the air. I turned to face the crowd—my hometown, my friends. Beaver Bluff was definitely not LA. It was a whole lot better.

Hamson's gaze rested on me, and his mouth tipped up a fraction. Despite Trudi attempting to wriggle out of his grasp, he leaned over and spoke in my ear, his breath tingling my skin. "Well, KC, it looks like you've done it again."

Chapter Twenty-Six

THE LOW-HANGING clouds and chill in the air weren't enough to stop the gang and me from celebrating Trudi's arrest with a barbecue. In fact, it was even better than the last time we'd solved a murder since the autumn leaves in the forest behind my house created a colorful backdrop. Not to mention the fact we had a few additions to our little group—Walter and David—now that they were no longer under suspicion.

David had arrived with a tub of potato salad.

The gang and I relaxed in my backyard while Pooh Bear and Bruno had endless fun coaxing each of us to play fetch. It was nice for Pooh to have a furry friend.

"These are the best ribs I've had since the turn of the century." Walter tucked into his rib with abandon while Naomi gazed at him adoringly from the seat next to him.

David dabbed his mouth with a napkin. "These are the *only* ribs I've ever had."

"What?" The gang and I gaped at him.

He shrugged. "Gran didn't really approve of messy foods."

Lulu patted her chest while flipping more ribs on the grill. "May she rest in peace."

We murmured our agreement. Oddly, I'd come to appreciate

Ruby more after her death than I had in life. Sure, she'd been difficult and demanding, but we all had our issues to deal with. Most of us were just doing the best we could with a little help from above.

"I guess in that case, we have a lot of foods for you to try." Verity waggled her eyebrows suggestively, never mind that she tended to hound *me* to stick to a training diet. (Not that either of us really ever did.)

David inched closer to her on the picnic bench, and they whispered together before Verity giggled and blushed.

"All right, you two. Dial it down a notch." Polly crossed her arms and smirked, though I had the sneaking suspicion she was just as happy for Verity and David's tentative new relationship as I was. But on the other hand, she didn't seem like such a fan of Naomi and Walter pairing up. I made a mental note to check on Polly more often, now that her sidekick would be occupied with a budding romance.

Lulu plated the ribs, then joined us at the table. "So, what finally happened with Trudi?"

In the twenty-four hours since the hullabaloo at Crumb's, a lot. I decided to go back to the beginning of what I knew for everyone's benefit. But not until I took another savory bite, the tang of the sauce filling my senses. It was almost enough to make me forget all my bumps and bruises, still tender to the touch. "Apparently, after Officers Leon and Kirby were the ones to haul Trudi away, and she broke down and made a confession on the way to the station."

"How'd you find that out?" Naomi nibbled at her potato salad.

"Officer Hamson called Crumb's after you guys left when I was still putting a few things away yesterday." I thought back to the call, and my heart slipped a little.

He hadn't even called my cell phone—not that he'd ever asked for my number. But according to Verity, you could find just about everything if you wanted to. The question was, why was my heart pulled towards Hamson? And why was he sending mixed signals? Next time I saw him, I'd confront him with it and ask him to shoot straight with me, even if it meant he didn't feel the same powerful attraction.

I offered Pooh Bear some of my food and was rewarded with a nuzzle. "Hamson said that Trudi had been next door at the outdoor shop buying rope, which they already knew based on security footage."

"I knew they had access to things that would've helped us sooner." Polly stuffed a bite into her mouth and chewed with a vengeance.

"I think we all knew that," Lulu chimed in.

"But we knew things they didn't, like about Ruby cutting someone out of her will." I took a sip of soda. Pooh Bear laid his head on my lap to beg another bite, which I happily gave. "It's like they worked on solving the crime based on evidence they found at the scene, and we were working it based on finding information about her life. I'm just glad I was right about my hunch since we didn't have definitive proof."

David released a sad sigh. "Doing both methods at the same time would've been faster."

"With the state fellas coming in and the force stretched thin, maybe that was all they could do." Walter tossed a food scrap to Bruno.

"Good point," David ceded.

Lulu wheeled her hand. "Back to the rope."

"Right, rope." I took a swig of soda and carefully chose my words so as not to hurt David with frank talk. "Like I said, Trudi had dropped in to buy rope and a few other things that she needed for the animal rescue, then when the gun went off and people left, she wandered next door and found Ruby alone. Apparently, she knew what the meeting was for and didn't like it."

Verity rubbed David's arm, and he offered a sad smile.

"By the way," David said, "Trudi was the daughter of one of Gran's friends, which I found out last night when I started digging around at home. Grandma only ever referred to this person as Ermantrude, which was why I'd never connected the dots, even when I went to the rescue and got Bruno."

I waited for the murmurs of support from the group to die down before I continued. "While everyone else was across the street with the gunshot victim, Trudi took her opportunity. Then, she left the back way, and no one was the wiser."

Everyone sat quietly for a few moments, and only the rustling of the leaves sounded in the forest behind us. Finally, Naomi spoke. "Walter, whatever happened to the guy who shot the gun?"

"Who, Charlie?" Walter offered a quiet chuckle. "The bullet nicked his foot, but he's doing all right. I think he had more to fear from his wife over him showing off with the gun than from the gun itself."

"Well, I don't blame her," Naomi said matter-of-factly. "Guns can be dangerous. You'd never do anything so dumb, would you?" She gazed up at Walter.

He snapped his suspenders. "Of course not—at least, not with a smart woman at my side."

The gang gave them both a good teasing, and then more pleasant conversation took over as they helped me clean up. After a few rousing games of cornhole, the barbecue petered out, and everyone went home. As Pooh Bear and I stood on the porch and watched the last car drive away, my heart was full.

Beaver Bluff was starting to feel like home again.

AN HOUR LATER, Pooh Bear and I nestled on the couch while I scrolled around on my tablet. With one major event out of the way, I could start to focus on my clients. A little side work would be a nice way to stay busy.

Pooh Bear's ears perked up a few seconds before I heard a vehicle outside. It wasn't yet dark, but late enough that I wasn't sure who would be dropping by. I peeked through the blinds, and my heart took off like a rocket—Hamson.

He strolled up the walkway wearing jeans that fit just so and an untucked flannel shirt layered over a tee. He ran his hand over his dark hair moments before he reached the porch, looking like a male model on one of the many photoshoots I'd been on in my previous life. Only those guys had nothing on Hamson.

Then he looked right at me. "I see you watching."

I dropped the blinds and smoothed down my hair. I wished I was wearing something besides old yoga pants and a tank, just like I wore every night to bed. I drew a fortifying breath and opened the door. "Officer, what brings you by?"

Hamson gazed at me, then down at the gash in the door, then back at me. "What happened?"

"Oh, that?" I opened the door wider and stood in front of it. "Nothing."

"You're a terrible liar, KC."

"I'll take that as a compliment." I smiled sweetly.

"In fact," he said, pointing to the door, "that's part of the reason I came by."

"Really?" I stepped aside. "Why? I mean, would you like to come inside?"

Pooh Bear looked at him warily.

Hamson offered his hand to Pooh, quickly passing the sniff test. "I think I will, thanks."

I gestured to the couch, but he waited for me to sit first before he situated himself. Pooh Bear jumped onto the spot between us. "So…you're here because of my door?"

Hamson flashed a confident grin. "In a manner of speaking. It looks like Trudi confessed to a couple of other things since yesterday."

"You mean…" I pointed to my face.

"Yes—and leaving a note on your door." He cleared his throat and gave me a stern look. Then he shook his head and spoke in a somber tone. "Why didn't you tell me?"

I bit my lip and looked away while trying to conjure a sufficient answer. In the end, I opted for the truth. "Because I figured you'd be mad."

Hamson leaned close enough for me to catch the scent of his aftershave. "KC, if you're in danger, I need to know. Maybe if you'd told me, Trudi wouldn't have assaulted you in the parking lot."

"Or maybe she would have. We can't play the what-if game." I picked a loose thread on my shirt.

"KC, look at me." He reached over and tipped my chin, eliciting a warning grunt from Pooh Bear. Hamson made sure I met his gaze before he continued. "This is the second time you've gotten involved in a case, despite my warning. Murder is dangerous. This isn't some mystery novel or TV show where the amateur sleuth always wins in the end. Things could have been so much worse."

My chin tingled from his touch. I swallowed all the words I wanted to say but couldn't. There was no reason I should have strong feelings for Hamson, not this soon. My heart was playing tricks on me. "If you cared so much, why didn't you come see me in the hospital?" I braced myself for his answer.

Hamson's jaw ticked, and he raked his hand through his hair while breathing deeply. "Right after you were assaulted at the gym, I went in and demanded to see the security footage, and when they didn't immediately show it to me, I started questioning people and looking for the perp." He breathed deeply and paused for a few moments.

I fidgeted, trying to take in everything Hamson was saying without interrupting him with a thousand questions that rushed through my head.

"When I got to the station, I was in a lot of trouble for the way I handled things, which was why I was hesitant to get involved when you came and asked me." He hooked into my gaze. "And that's why I have to be careful now."

I closed my eyes and went for it. "Does that mean you're interested, then?"

Hamson tipped my chin again, this time stopping to caress my cheek. Slowly, I opened my eyes to meet his dark gaze as my body hummed with anticipation.

Moments passed before he spoke. "Trust me, I'm very interested. The truth is, I just don't know how this all plays out."

"Do we have to know how it plays out?"

"Aside from my job, from what I've heard, you plan to head back to the city the first chance you get." Hamson sat back on the couch.

"Well, maybe not the *first* chance."

Hamson laughed, his smile lighting the room. "I guess it wouldn't hurt to hang out a little more."

"Even with my stripey hair?" I asked, recalling his face when he'd seen me after the salon fiasco.

"Yeah, even with stripey hair." He flashed another grin, his dimples deepening. "Besides, I'm more interested in that sharp brain of yours."

"Oh, is that so?" I teased. "Would that be my keen crime-solving brain?"

Hamson groaned. "We're going to have to have some boundaries—definite boundaries. You have to stay out of police business. I'd like to keep my job."

"Fine, I can agree to that." I stroked Pooh Bear's fur to hide my trembling hands. "It's not like we'll keep finding dead bodies here in Beaver Bluff."

Hamson's hand met mine atop Pooh's back. "Now, I have a little surprise for you outside."

"Let's go see." Excitement lit inside me as I hopped off the couch. "I can't even imagine what it could be."

"A little birdie told me something you wanted." Hamson and Pooh Bear followed me outside.

"Would the birdie's name be Verity?"

"Actually, no." Hamson scooted past me and opened the door of his truck. Gently, he scooped out a ball of golden fur.

"Cujo!" I hurried to his side and drew the pup to my chest. "Oh, look at you, you tiny, little love." I stroked his fur and cuddled him closely.

Pooh Bear barked.

"Naughty boy. Stop that." I admonished Pooh softly so as not to scare Cujo. Then I looked up at Hamson, who hovered by our sides. "How did you know?"

"Believe it or not, Trudi told me you had a special connection with this little guy, and she wanted to see him go to a good home." He shrugged, seemingly as baffled as I was by the two distinct faces of Trudi. "But if he's not a good fit because of Pooh Bear, then we can figure something out."

I liked how he said we. I smiled up at him, drinking in the sight of Hamson's silhouette at sunset. Hopefully, the first of many sunsets to come. "Thank you. I'm sure Pooh will learn to enjoy the company." I leaned into Hamson for a tentative hug.

A car honked, breaking us apart.

I drew back, uncertain who else would show up at this time. The car pulled to the curb and came into focus. Not just any car, a zillion-dollar sports car.

Adrenaline slammed through my veins as the driver emerged, peeling off sunglasses that were completely unnecessary this time of evening. "Hey there, KC." He held out his hands. "Aren't you going to say hello?"

I shook my head as reality crashed over me, and all I could do was utter his name. "James."

THE END

✳✳✳

Thank you for spending time with the gang and me in Beaver

Bluff! If you enjoyed our time together, please leave a review so others can discover KC Crumb and her posse.

Would you like to read more about the Beaver Bluff crew? Sign up for my newsletter at georgianadaniels.com/newsletter and I'll send you a free short story prequel called *The Mystery of the Missing Groom* as a thank you.

Watch out for book 3, *A Crummy Way to Die*, coming in 2022!

You can find me on Facebook, Bookbub, and Goodreads. Or you can also drop me a line at georgiana@georgianadaniels.com

Acknowledgments

Behind every great book, there's a village of people who poured their time, expertise, love, and friendship into the author. Looking at all the people who have come alongside to help me, or simply put up with my craziness over the last few years, I realize how blessed I am!

Betsy Haddox, you are the world's best crit buddy and friend! I would never have made it this long without your encouragement, cyber coffee, fun memes, and daily Voxes. You are the best of the best!

Jaci Norton and Liz Winney, I appreciate the time you offered me by beta reading this book and offering your insights. I love you ladies!

Dineen Miller, you are the best cover designer ever! I look forward to seeing you in person again someday for more love and laughs.

Many thanks to Kristin Avila for your editing talent. Thank you for saving me from myself and my fondness for crazy punctuation.

Go Team Crumbs! Thank you for giving your time and energy to help spread the word about *Crumb and Punishment*. I appreciate each one of you so very much.

Last but certainly not least, thank you to my family. You've helped me in countless ways with your silent (and vocal) support. My parents George and Tessie Moate, dear hubby Troy Daniels, and daughters Mallory Cornelius, Chloe Daniels, and Tori Daniels—you are a treasure from God. He must love me to pair me up with you guys! Thanks for everything, a million times over.

www.ingramcontent.com/pod-product-compliance
Lightning Source LLC
Chambersburg PA
CBHW021327190726
48288CB00003B/993